"Don't get scared and bolt, schoolgirl. I won't attack you."

Carla's head came up proudly. "I never thought you would."

"You must have thought it once," Luke shot back. "Because you ran like hell and stayed away for three years."

She turned away, gazing out over September Canyon. "That was humiliation, not fear," she said finally. "I was naive enough to believe I had something to offer you."

He looked at her for a long moment, his mouth tight with anger and pain. "I've regretted that night like I've regretted nothing else in my life."

She turned back to him, a wondering kind of surprise in her blue-green eyes. "Why? Why do you regret what happened?"

For a long time there was only silence. And the sinuous dance of fire and rain.

"It was the sweetest offer I've ever had," he said. "I wanted you that night until I shook with it.... I've wanted you like that for years."

ELIZABETH LOWELL

FIRE AND RAIN

Silhouette Books

Published by Silhouette Books

America's Publisher of Contemporary Romance

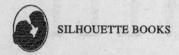

SILHOUETTE BOOKS

ISBN 0-373-48399-6

FIRE AND RAIN

Visit us at www.romance.net

Printed in U.S.A.

To Michael...
Wherever you are.

1

What in hell am I doing here?

Luke looked in the mirror, swiped a last bit of axle grease off his chin and had no fast answers for his silent question. In fact, he had no answer at all as to why he had stayed on at Cash McQueen's apartment knowing that Carla McQueen was coming to dinner.

It wasn't unusual for Luke to drive the long miles between his ranch in Four Corners country and the city of Boulder in order to visit his friend Cash. It wasn't unusual for the two of them to take on some kind of repair work on Cash's balky Jeep. It wasn't unusual for the two of them to split a pizza and a six-pack afterward and catch up on mutual news.

It was damned unusual that Carla would appear in the same room with Luke MacKenzie.

Is that why Cash dodged my question about who Carla is dating? Luke asked his reflection in the mirror. *Did she finally get over me and say yes to*

*some nice city boy? And what business is it of mine
if she did?*

Even as he tried to tell himself that it was only
natural that he have a big-brotherly concern for the
little sister of his best friend, Luke knew that was
only part of the truth. The rest of the truth was a
steel spur digging into his self-esteem: three years
ago he had wanted Carla so badly that he had sent
her running for her life from the Rocking M.

And him.

With an effort, Luke forced aside the image of
Carla's wide blue-green eyes and trembling lips and
the soft heat of her body flowing over his. That image had come to too many of his dreams, waking or
sleeping. But that wasn't what he wanted from her.
It sure as hell wasn't what he would take from her.
What he wanted, all he would accept, was a return
to the days when they had shared the kind of companionship Luke hadn't known was possible with a
woman.

*It's been three years. Surely Carla's forgotten the
whole thing by now. Surely she and Cash and I can
be an almost family again, the way we used to be.*

*God, I've missed the sound of her laughter and
the way her smile used to light up the whole house.*

"Hey, Luke, are you taking root in there?"

"I'm still trying to get your Jeep out from under
my fingernails," Luke retorted to Cash. "You ought
to trade that damn thing for a dog and shoot the
dog."

The bathroom door opened. Cash's big body filled the frame with little left over.

"Give me your shirt," Cash said.

"Why?"

"The Jeep drooled all down your spine."

Luke made a sound of disgust that Cash didn't take seriously. But then, neither did Luke.

"The things I do for you," Luke muttered.

With quick, deft movements he rinsed his hands, stripped off the black shirt and fired it at Cash's head. Another shirt came flying back at the same speed. Luke pulled it on with a small smile; the shirt fit as well as one of his own. Cash was the only man Luke knew whose clothes he could wear without feeling as though he were in a straitjacket.

"Much better," Cash said. "Can't have you looking like something the cat dragged in and didn't eat. What would Carla think?"

"She's seen me looking worse."

"Not on her twenty-first birthday. Hurry up. I can't decorate cake worth a damn."

"What makes you think I can?"

"Desperation."

Grinning, Luke tucked in the shirt and followed Cash to the kitchen, feeling very much at home. In many ways Carla and Cash were as close to a real family as Luke had ever come. His mother, like his grandmother and great-grandmother before her, had hated the Rocking M. Even worse, his mother had feared the land and the wind as though they were alive and hunting her. Finally she had had a nervous breakdown. Her parents had swept in from the East Coast, picked up the pieces of their daughter and removed her from the Rocking M. They had also taken Luke's seven-year-old sister, whom he loved as he hadn't permitted himself to love anything since. Neither mother nor sister had ever been heard from since that day.

At thirteen, Luke had been left alone with a silent, hard-drinking father and a ranch whose demands were as endless as the land itself was beautiful. At nineteen he had inherited the Rocking M. At twenty he had hired Cash to do a resources survey of the ranch. Six months later Cash had shown up for the summer with his half sister, a sad-eyed waif whose attempts at smiles had broken Luke's heart. Perhaps it was the memory of his own little sister, perhaps it was Carla's haunting eyes, perhaps it was only his own need to protect and care for something more gentle than himself. Whatever the reason, Carla had slipped past defenses Luke didn't even know he had.

One day while riding a distant corner of the ranch, he had found a shard of ancient Anasazi pottery in September Canyon. He had given the piece of the past to Carla, trying to tell her that nothing is lost forever, that everyone is part of what came before and what will come after. Somehow she had understood all that he couldn't find words for, and she had cried for the first time since her parents had died. He had held her, feeling her trust as she gave herself to his strength and wept until she couldn't lift her head. And as he held her, he felt as though he himself were crying for all that he had lost when he had been about Carla's age.

"Yo, Luke," Cash said, snapping his fingers in front of the other man's whiskey-colored eyes. "Anybody home?"

Luke grunted. "Where's the cake?"

"Over there."

"I was afraid you were going to say that." Luke sighed as he looked at a lopsided chocolate heap that was charred on the sides and sticky in the middle. "Hope you made a bucket of icing."

"It's in the sink."

Luke glanced over at the sink. There was, indeed, a white substance in the sink. No bowl. Just sink.

"Tell you what," Luke drawled. "Why don't I bring the cake over, mess it around a bit and then turn on the garbage disposal?"

"I have candles," Cash said indignantly.

"Stick them in the ice cream."

"C'mon, *hombre*. Where's your sense of adventure? If we use the soup ladle for the icing, maybe we won't drip too much on the floor."

Luke was dumping the first load of icing on the cake when he heard Carla's voice call from the front door.

"Open up, big brother! My hands are full."

"Happy birthday, sis," Cash said, opening the

door. "Look who's here. He just happened to—watch it!"

Luke had a glimpse of shocked, blue-green eyes, then Carla was grabbing frantically for the limp pizza box she had been in the process of handing over to Cash when she had spotted Luke.

"Nice catch, schoolgirl," Luke drawled, watching Carla with a masculine hunger he would never admit, because there was nothing he would permit himself to do to assuage that hunger.

Except look at her. He allowed himself to do that, his eyes cataloguing every feature. Sun-streaked chestnut hair, eyes like pieces of the sea, a body whose curves she never flaunted—but they were there just the same, a promise of heat that had made him ache since she was sixteen. With the ease of long practice, Luke shunted his thoughts aside, concentrating on seeing Carla as what she was: his best friend's kid sister.

"Pizza tastes better when you don't have to comb it out of the rug with your teeth," Luke pointed out.

"I'll take your word for it," Carla said, as though it had been a day rather than almost a year since she had been this close to Luke. "I'm partial to plates and tables myself."

"You used to be more adventurous."

Luke saw the words slip past Carla's cool, tightly held surface and knew as clearly as if she had shouted it that she was remembering what had happened three years before, the night she had graduated from high school, stood in front of him and declared her love.

Most nights Luke might have been able to smile and send Carla on her way feeling no more than a little embarrassed for her sweet declaration. But it hadn't been most other nights. It had been one of the nights when his elemental hunger for Cash's little sister had driven Luke to the temporary relief of straight Scotch. Instead of turning away from her, he had come to his feet, grabbed her and kissed her with every bit of the wild hunger in him. When she had tried to slow him down, to talk to him, he had lashed out.

What did you think a man wanted from a woman who loves him, school girl? And there's the problem, isn't it? You're a girl mouthing woman's words and I'm a man on fire. Run, school girl. Run like hell and don't come back.

Carla had taken Luke at his word. She had run and she hadn't come back. And he had locked himself up in the barn with his tools, transforming his yearnings into gleaming shapes of wood—chair and dresser, headboard and footboard, beautiful furnishings for the dream that could not come true.

"Ah, well, live and learn," Carla said.

"What have you learned, sunshine?" Luke asked.

He saw the ripple of emotion in her clear eyes as he called her by the old nickname. But the emotion passed, and she was again watching him with the combination of distance and coolness that she had used on him whenever she couldn't avoid him.

"I've learned that being adventurous is another name for being a fool," she said.

Luke saw the tiny flinch she couldn't conceal and knew that he had hurt her. He hadn't really intended that. He had just wanted to see something besides aloofness and distance in her beautiful eyes.

"You've got no corner on being a fool," Luke said calmly. "Seems like all I do lately is chase stubborn cows and eat bad food." He yawned and stretched his arms over his head, flattening his palms on the ceiling in order to fully stretch his body.

"Get a cook," Carla said, walking past Luke to the kitchen.

As he lowered his arms, his fingertips accidentally brushed over her arm and her glossy, shoulder-length hair. The short-sleeved blouse she wore couldn't conceal the sudden ripple of goose bumps, helpless response to his touch.

"I've had six cooks in the past twenty months," Luke said. "Not a one of them could hold a candle to you. I've missed all those dinners when you and Cash and I would sit and talk about everything and nothing, and then Cash and I would fight over who got the biggest piece of whatever pie you'd made that day. Those were good times, sunshine."

Carla's hands gripped the pizza box too tightly. She slapped the box onto the counter and began transferring slices to a baking sheet.

"Bet you don't miss doing the dishes afterward," she said.

"The conversation was worth it," Luke said simply.

"Oh, no you don't," Cash said.

"I don't what?" Luke asked.

"You don't come sniffing around looking to make Carla your cook for the summer, leaving me with a can opener for company."

Luke smiled slowly. "Hell of an idea, Cash. Sunshine, would you—"

"Nope," Carla said quickly, interrupting.

"Why not?"

Ignoring him, Carla bent over the open stove and positioned the limp pizza as though it were a gear in a Swiss watch.

"Why not?" Luke pressed.

"Cash would starve, that's why," she muttered.

"Slander! I can cook as well as the next man," Cash said.

"Sure," she retorted, "as long as the next man is Luke MacKenzie."

Before either man could speak, Carla spotted the brown-and-white mess at the end of the counter. Cautiously she dipped her finger in a thin white puddle that had formed on the tile next to the battered cake. Luke's eyes followed the tip of her tongue as she tasted the goo on her finger.

"Too sweet for gravy or paint," she said after a moment, giving Cash a teasing sideways glance. She stirred the puddle with her fingertip, noted that the white stuck to everything except the brown mound it had been poured over, and smiled. "I do believe my brother has invented a fairly tasty form of library paste."

Luke snickered.

"Slander," Cash said, trying not to smile. "Is that why you turned down my kind offer to cook and insisted on bringing pizza instead?"

"Bingo," Carla said.

"Which reminds me, how much do I owe you for the pizza?"

"A hundred dollars."

Carla's tone was so casual that it took a few instants for the amount to sink in.

Cash did a double take and asked, "What's on that pizza—beluga caviar?"

"Pepperoni and mushrooms. I included the birthday present I knew you'd be too busy chasing rocks to get for me."

"Oh. What did I get you?"

"A few more weeks with Fred."

"Fred?" Luke said before he could stop himself. "Who the hell is Fred?"

2

"Fred's a what," Carla said.

"Huh?"

"Now you're getting the idea," she murmured.

Luke's eyes narrowed.

"Fred's her baby," Cash added unhelpfully.

"Do tell," Luke retorted. "And soon, I hope."

Carla fought against the smile she felt stealing over her lips, but couldn't stifle it any more than she could prevent the helpless yearning that went through her when Luke smiled approvingly at her in return. He hadn't changed. He was still tall, powerful, intense. His very dark brown hair set off his amber eyes, making them look gold in certain kinds of light. The trace of beard shadow beneath his high cheekbones perfectly suited his hard-jawed Slavic features.

For a moment it felt as though time had turned back upon itself, touching again the years before she had mistaken Luke's affectionate tolerance for a very different kind of love. Longing swept through her, a futile wish that she had been different three years ago, or he had been; but she hadn't, and he hadn't, and the memories still shook her. She saw Luke as she had seen him that night, a huge, looming presence, his eyes a golden blaze of reflected firelight. The width of his shoulders had blocked out the world when he bent down and swept her up in an embrace.

The first instants had been pure bliss, the culmination of years and years of dreaming; and then his arms had tightened and tightened and tightened until she couldn't breathe. His mouth had become rough and demanding, forcing hers to open, giving her a kiss that was as hard and adult as the male body grinding intimately against hers. She had been confused, completely at a loss, and finally a little frightened. It wasn't how she had envisioned Luke's response to her declaration of love—where was the tenderness, the joy, the sweetness of knowing you loved and were loved in return?

With an effort, Carla banished the agonizing memories and answered Luke's question. "Fred is my truck."

"Tell him the truth," advised Cash. "Fred is a battered, bewildered, dwarf four-by-four that does its best to play with the big boys. I can't tell you how many times I've gotten a call and had to go and winch Carla out of some damned mud hole. Next time it happens I've got half a mind to make *you* go and get her, Luke. After all, it's all your fault that she's barreling all over the Four Corners chasing ancient shadows.''

Luke's intent, golden eyes fixed on Cash. "It is?"

"Damned straight. If you hadn't given her that shard of Anasazi pottery you found somewhere up in September Canyon, she never would have become interested in archaeology. If she weren't interested in archaeology, she wouldn't have been off running after old bones with her professors every summer and most vacations."

"I thought it was boys that girls chased," Luke said, fixing Carla with enigmatic golden eyes.

"I gave up chasing boys right after I graduated from high school," Carla said flatly. "And stop trying to change the subject," she continued, turning to Cash, changing the subject herself. "You owe me fourteen bucks for the pizza."

"And eighty-six bucks for truck repairs?"

She smiled slightly and shook her head. "No, but I wouldn't turn down a hug."

Cash engulfed Carla in a hug. Though she was five foot seven, the top of her head barely brushed Cash's chin. He lifted her and swung her around. When he set her down again, she was almost on Luke's feet. There was barely room for her to breathe. Luke was the same height as her brother, six foot three, and weighed within a pound or two of Cash's one ninety-six. That was probably one of the reasons the two men got along so well—they were built on the same scale. Big.

Without warning, Luke's long fingers tilted Carla's chin, forcing her to meet his eyes.

"Are you really all grown-up now, sunshine?"

The old nickname and the searching intensity of Luke's eyes took Carla's breath away, making speech impossible.

"Hey, that reminds me," Cash said. "It's been months since I've played killer poker."

"Not surprising," Luke retorted, releasing Carla with the speed of a man passing a hot potato on to its final destination. "It's been months since you've found an out-of-state sucker who doesn't know why Alexander McQueen is called 'Cash.'"

"Lucky at cards, unlucky at love."

Luke snorted. "I'll shuffle. Carla can deal. You open the champagne I brought."

"Champagne?" Carla asked, stunned.

She looked up into Luke's eyes. He was still standing close to her, so close that she could sense the heat of his big body. She hadn't sensed anyone's presence so acutely in years.

Three years, to be exact.

Luke's slow smile as he looked down at Carla made something stir and shimmer to life deep within her.

"Champagne," he confirmed, his voice deep. "You only turn twenty-one once. It should be special."

By the time the cards were shuffled, cut and dealt, Carla was sipping from a glass of golden champagne, which fizzed and sizzled softly over her lips and tongue. She hardly noticed the alcohol, for her blood was already sparkling from the memory of Luke's fingers on her skin.

Are you really all grown-up now?

The implications of that question scattered Carla's attention, making her lose at cards more rapidly than usual. Before Luke poured her a second glass of champagne, she had lost her original stake—six dollars. She handed over the last of her nickels without rancor, for it had been Cash rather than Luke who had won the lion's share of the pots. Long ago, Carla had decided that Cash must have made a deal with the devil in exchange for luck at cards.

By the time Luke poured Carla a third glass of champagne, the pizza was reduced to grease spots on the paper plates, and it had become clear to everyone that Cash's luck was running as high as ever. Luke was down to three dollars from his original six, and Carla had traded seven days' worth of home-cooked meals for fifty cents each and promptly had lost every penny.

Normally Carla would have stopped drinking halfway through her second glass of champagne, but nothing about her twenty-first birthday was normal—especially the presence of Luke MacKenzie. The champagne was a dancing delight that smelled as yeasty as the bread she loved to bake. Cash and

Luke were in fine form, trading insults and laughter equally. When Luke poured a third glass of champagne for Carla, she was into Cash for a summer's worth of meals and Luke was down to seventy-five cents.

Carla rooted for Cash unabashedly, frankly enjoying seeing Luke on the losing end of something for a change. Luke took the "card lessons" in good humor, squeezing every bit of mileage from his shrinking pile of small change.

And then slowly, almost imperceptibly, Luke started winning. He rode the unexpected streak of luck aggressively, repeatedly betting everything he had and getting twice as much back from the pot. By the time the last drops from the magnum of champagne had been poured—by Carla into Luke's glass, in a blatant attempt to fuzz his mind—Cash was down to his last nickel. He tossed it into the pot philosophically, calling Luke's most recent raise.

Luke fanned out his cards to reveal a pair of sevens, nine high. Cash made a disgusted sound and threw in his hand without showing his cards.

"What?" Carla said in disbelief. She reached for Cash's abandoned cards, only to have her fingers lightly slapped by her brother.

"Bad dog, drop!" he teased. "You know the rules. It costs good money to see those cards and you're broke."

Carla withdrew her fingers and muttered, "I still

don't believe that you couldn't crawl over a lousy pair of sevens."

"You forgot the nine," Luke said.

"It's easy to forget something that small," Carla shot back. She sighed. "Well, I guess this just wasn't your night, big brother. All you won was something you would have gotten anyway—a summer's worth of dinners cooked by yours truly."

"Sounds like a damned good deal to me," Luke said.

There was a moment of silence, followed by another. The silence stretched. Luke arched his dark eyebrows at Cash in silent query. Cash smiled.

"You'll have to throw in wages," Cash said.

"Same as I paid the last housekeeper. But she'll have to keep house, too. For that I'd bet everything on the table. One hand. Winner take all."

"What do you say, sis?" Cash asked, turning toward Carla.

"Huh?"

"Luke has agreed to bet everything in the pot against your agreement to be the Rocking M's cook and housekeeper."

"You're out of school for the summer, right?" Luke asked.

She nodded, too off balance to tell him that she was out of school, period. She had crammed four years of studying in the three years since she had graduated from high school. It had been the perfect excuse not to spend summers on the Rocking M, as she had since she was fourteen.

"You can start next weekend and go until the end of August. A hundred days, give or take a few," Luke said casually, but his eyes had the predatory intensity of a bird of prey. "Room, board and wages, same as for any hired hand."

Carla stared at Cash. He smiled encouragingly. She tried to think of all the reasons she would be a raving idiot for taking the bet.

Her blood sizzled softly, champagne and something more.

"Do you have your toes crossed for luck?" Carla demanded of her brother.

"Yep."

She took a deep breath. "Go for it."

Cash turned to Luke. "Five cards, no discard, no draw, nothing wild. Best hand wins."

"Deal," Luke said.

Suddenly it was so quiet that the sound of the cards being shuffled was like muffled thunder. The slap of cards on the table was distinct, rhythmic. There was the ritual exchange of words, the discreet fanning and survey of five cards. Luke's expression was impossible to read as he laid his hand faceup on the table and said neutrally, "Ace high...and nothing else. Not a damned thing."

Cash swore and swiftly gathered all the cards together into an indistinguishable pile. "You're shot with luck tonight, Luke. All I had was a jack."

For an instant there was silence. Then Luke began laughing. When he turned and saw Carla's stunned face, his expression changed.

"When the isolation gets to you," Luke said carefully, "I'll let you welsh on the bet. No hard feelings and no regrets."

"What?"

"Women hate the Rocking M," Luke said simply. "I doubt that you'll last three weeks, much less three months. College has made a city slicker out of you. Two weekends without bright lights and you'll be whining and pining like all the other housekeepers and cooks did. You can make book on it."

Whining and pining.

The words echoed in Carla's mind, leaving a bright, irrational anger in their wake.

"You're on, cowboy," she said flatly. "What's more, you're going to eat every last one of your words. Raw."

"Doubt it."

"I don't. I'm going to be the one who feeds them to you."

Luke's slow smile doubled Carla's heart rate and set fire to her nerve endings. He laughed a soft, rough kind of laugh and gave her the only warning she would get.

"There's something to remember when you start feeding me, baby."

"What's that?"

"I bite."

3

What in God's name am I doing here? Have I gone entirely crazy?

"Here" was on a dirt road winding and looping and climbing up to the Rocking M. All around Carla for mile upon uninhabited mile, the Four Corners countryside lay in unbridled magnificence. It wasn't the absence of people that was causing Carla to question her own sanity; she loved the rugged, wild land. It was the presence of people that was giving her stomach the ohmygod flutters. To be precise, it was the presence of one particular person—Luke MacKenzie, owner of a handsome chunk of the surrounding land.

And a handsome chunk himself.

In the back of her mind Carla kept hearing her brother's advice. *Chin up, Carla. You can do anything for a summer. Besides, you heard Luke. He won't be any harder on you than he is on any other ranch hand.*

"Thanks, big brother," Carla muttered as she remembered Cash's smiling send-off that morning. "Thanks all to hell."

Not that she was angry with Cash for being amused by her predicament. He had only been doing what big brothers always did, which was to treat their smaller sisters with a combination of mischief, indulgence and love. Nor was it Cash's fault that Carla found herself driving over a rough road to a live-in summer job with the man who had haunted her dreams for every one of the seven years since she had been fourteen. Cash wasn't at fault because he hadn't been the one to suggest the bet that he had ultimately lost.

However, he had neglected to mention that Luke would be part of her birthday celebration. When Carla walked in the front door and saw him, she had nearly dropped the pizza she was carrying. Luke had always had that effect on her. When he was nearby, her normal composure evaporated. She had made a fool of herself around him throughout her teenage years.

Well, not quite all of my teenage years, Carla told herself bracingly. *I was eighteen when I took the cure. Or rather, when Luke administered it.*

After that, she had stopped finding excuses to go out to the Rocking M and watch the man she loved. But she hadn't stopped soon enough. She hadn't stopped before she had told Luke that she loved him and begged him to look at her as a woman, not a girl.

The memory of that disastrous evening still had the ability to make Carla flush, go pale and then flush again with a volatile combination of emotions she had no desire to sort out or describe. The one emotion she had no trouble putting a name to was humiliation. She had been mortified to the soles of her feet. But she had learned something useful that night. She had learned that people didn't die of embarrassment.

They just wanted to.

So she had turned and run from the scene of her personal Waterloo. Driving recklessly, crying, putting as much distance as she could between herself and the man who was much too sophisticated for her, she had fled the ranch. All the way home she had told herself that she hated Luke. She hadn't believed it, but she had wanted to.

Since then, Carla had tried to put Luke Mac-Kenzie out of her mind. She hadn't succeeded. Every time she went out on a date, she only missed Luke more. Not surprisingly, she didn't date much. The harder she tried to find other men attractive, the brighter Luke's image burned in her memory.

No man can be that special, Carla told herself fiercely. *My memory isn't reliable. If I were around Luke now, as a woman, he wouldn't be nearly so attractive to me. Familiarity breeds contempt. That's*

*why I let all this happen. I wanted to get familiar
enough to feel contempt.*

That, or outright insanity, was the only explanation
for what had happened the evening of her
twenty-first birthday, a celebration of the very date
when she had legally become old enough to know
better.

*Look on the bright side. A summer on the Rocking
M beats a summer as a gofer for the Department of
Archaeology. If I have to check one more reference
on one more footnote, I'll do something rash.*

*Get used to it. That's what being an archaeologist
is all about.*

While learning about vanished cultures and peoples
fascinated Carla, she wasn't certain that a career
as an archaeologist was what she wanted. She was
certain that she was going to find out; she would
begin work on her master's degree in the fall. But
first she had to get through the summer. And Luke.

Carla's mind was still seething with silent questions
when she drove into the Rocking M's ranch
yard, got out slowly and stretched. She was presently
just under three and one half hours from the
bright lights of Cortez, assuming that the weather
continued fair and clear. In bad weather, she was
anywhere between six and sixty hours from "civilization."

The isolation didn't bother her. In fact, it was a
positive lure; she had always felt drawn to the wide,
wild sweep of the land. After she had turned sev-

enteen, the only serious arguments she and her brother had ever had was over her tendency to go from camp with a canteen, a compass, and a backpack, and leave behind a note and an arrow made of pebbles to indicate the direction of her exploration. The fact that Cash did precisely the same thing didn't lessen his anger at Carla; in Cash's book, what was sauce for the goose was *not* sauce for the gander. When Carla had gone to Luke looking for sympathy, he had calmly told her that he didn't want her going alone anywhere on the ranch, including the pasture across the road from the big house.

Carla's mouth turned up slightly at the memory. She had been furious when the two men had ganged up against her. When she had started to point out that Luke was being unreasonable, he had told her that as long as she was on the Rocking M she would obey his orders. Period. End of discussion.

She hadn't argued. The next time she went into West Fork for supplies, she had started looking for work. That afternoon she got work as the cook and housekeeper for the OK Corral, a small motel-coffee shop at the edge of West Fork. The job included room and board. She had gone back to the Rocking M, unloaded the supplies, and started packing her clothes. When she was ready to leave, she went looking for Ten, Luke's ramrod. Ten had listened to her request, discovered where she was going to be working, and had gone to find Luke. Luke had flatly refused to let her use any of the ranch vehicles for any reason whatsoever, effectively imprisoning her on the Rocking M until Cash returned from his latest round of explorations.

Remembering the blowup that had followed made Carla's faint smile fade.

"Such a long face."

The sound of Luke's voice made Carla jump, for she had thought she was alone. She looked toward the long front porch of the ranch house. Luke was sitting in the shadows watching her. She couldn't help staring as he stood up, stepped off the porch and walked into the bright sunlight. It had been only a day since the card game in which she had lost her summer freedom, but she looked at Luke as though it had been a year since she had seen him.

Nothing about him had changed. Long-boned, hard, with a muscular grace that had always fascinated her, Luke overshadowed every other man she had ever known. He had haunted her, making boyfriends impossible. She could enjoy other students' company, pal around with them, go to shows or football games; but she simply couldn't take the boys seriously. When they wanted to go from friendship to something more intense, she gently, inevitably, withdrew.

Carla watched Luke walking toward her and prayed that her half-formed plan would work, that she would be able to get Luke out of her system, to cure herself of her futile longing for a man who didn't want her.

Not until Luke stood close enough for her to see that the sun had turned his eyes into clear, deep gold did Carla realize the true extent of her wager—and her risk. What if this didn't work? What if being close to Luke only increased her longing? What if this turned out to be as big a mistake as her job in West Fork had been?

"Already unhappy at being stuck in the sticks for a few months?" Luke continued, watching Carla closely.

"No. I was thinking about the summer I got a job at the OK Corral."

Luke's eyes narrowed and his mouth became a thin line. Carla winced.

"You got off easy," he said flatly. "If you'd been my sister, I would have nailed your backside to the barn for a stunt like that."

"Cash is brighter than that."

"Or dumber."

"Maybe he decided that teaching me wilderness skills was better than having me move out."

"Not just 'out,' schoolgirl. Into a no-tell motel."

"A what?"

"The OK Corral is the biggest hot-sheet operation this side of Cortez."

"Hot sheet?" she asked. Suddenly understanding dawned. "You don't mean…?"

"I sure as hell do."

"Oh…my…God."

Carla's blue-green eyes widened in comprehension. Amused by her own naïveté, she shook her head slowly, making light twist through her sun-streaked chestnut hair. Unable to hold back any longer, she let laughter bubble up. She finally understood why Luke had kept her a virtual prisoner on the ranch until Cash had come in from his geological explorations three days later.

As Luke watched Carla, his mouth gentled into a smile. Something that was both pain and pleasure expanded through him. It had been so good during the years when he and Cash had shared between them the radiant freshness that was Carla. She had a way of brightening everything she touched. Luke hadn't wanted to let Carla go out into the world any more than Cash had. The world could be brutal to a gentle young girl.

So we kept her and then I was the one to teach her how brutal the world can be.

The thought made Luke's expression harden. The memory of Carla's frightened, tear-streaked face, the broken sounds she had made as she fled into the night three years before; all of it haunted him.

"Lord, sunshine," Luke said in a deeper voice. "You were so innocent. No wonder Cash wanted to build a fence around you to keep out the wolves."

Carla's laughter died as she looked at Luke and knew that he was thinking of the night she had thrown herself at him. She felt herself going pale, then flushing beneath a rising tide of embarrassment. She hated the revealing color but knew there was nothing she could do to avoid or conceal it. So she ignored it, just as she tried to ignore Luke's comment about her innocence, his words like salt on the raw wound of her memories.

Yet if she were to survive this summer—and Luke—the past had to be put behind her. She was a woman now, not a stupid girl blinded by naive dreams of being loved by a man who was years too experienced for her.

"Fortunately, innocence is curable," Carla said. "Time works miracles. Where do you want me to put my stuff?"

For an instant she held her breath, silently willing Luke to accept the change of subject. She really couldn't bear reliving the lowest moment of her life all over again. Not in front of Luke, with his intense glance measuring every bright shade of her humiliation.

"Sunshine, that night you came and—"

"My name is Carla," she interrupted tightly, turning away, going to the tiny bed of the pickup truck. "Do you want me to park at the old house?"

"No. You'll be staying at the big house."

"But—"

"But nothing. I'm not having anything as innocent as you running loose after dark. One of my hands is no good around women, and none of them is any better than he has to be. When Cash is here, you can bunk in with him at the old house if you want. Otherwise, you're in the big house with me.

It's hard to get men to work on a place as isolated as the Rocking M. I'd hate to have to drive one of my hands to the hospital because he was drinking and saw a light on in the old house and thought he'd try his luck.''

"None of your men would—''

"Didn't you learn anything three years ago?'' Luke cut in. "Men drink to forget, and one of the first things they forget is to keep their hands off an innocent girl like you.''

"I'm not an inno—''

"Put that suitcase back,'' Luke said coldly, interrupting Carla again.

"What?'' she asked, stopping in the act of taking a suitcase from the truck's small, open bed.

"I'm not going to spend the summer arguing with the hired help. If you can't take a simple order you can turn that toy truck around and get the hell off the Rocking M.''

Carla stared in disbelief at Luke. Hurt and anger warred within her.

"Would you treat me like this if Cash were here?''

"If Cash were here, I wouldn't have to worry about protecting you from your own foolishness. He'd take care of it for me.''

"I'm twenty-one, legally of age.''

"Schoolgirl, when it comes to men and an isolated ranch like this, you aren't even out of kindergarten. Take your pick—the big house or the road to town.''

Carla turned and began rummaging in the truck bed again. She hoped Luke couldn't see the tiny trembling of her hands at the thought of living in the same house with him, seeing him at all hours of light and darkness, fixing his food, making his bed, washing his clothes, folding them, caring for him. A thousand subtle intimacies, his whiskey-colored eyes watching her, no place to retreat, no place to hide.

Well, that's what I came here for, isn't it, to let familiarity breed contempt? And if the thought of that kind of closeness makes my knees turn to water, that's just tough. I'll get over him. I have to.

With all the coolness Carla could muster, she turned back to Luke. He said something harsh beneath his breath as he saw the pallor of her face and her wide, haunted eyes.

''Don't worry. I'm not going to jump your bones,'' he said savagely. ''Hell, I wouldn't have touched you three years ago if I hadn't been drinking and you hadn't been offering. Look at you, all pale and trembling every time the subject comes up. You'd think I raped you, for God's sake.''

''No,'' she said hoarsely. ''No.''

''Damn it, I'm not going to have you flinching and hiding every time I get three feet from you. Nothing happened that night!''

Hearing her declaration of love characterized as

"nothing" stiffened Carla's knees. Her head came up and she asked in a low voice, "Do you want a cook and housekeeper for the summer?"

"Yes, but—"

She kept right on talking. "Then what happened the summer I graduated from high school is off limits for conversation. It was the most excruciating, humiliating experience of my life. Thinking about it makes me—sick." Abruptly Carla stopped speaking and shook her head, making silky hair fly. "So unless you're trying to drive me off the ranch, you'll stop throwing that night in my face."

Being told that the memory of his touch sickened her did nothing to improve Luke's temper. He looked at Carla's tight, pale face and swore under his breath.

"It's too late to be hedging your bet," he said coldly. "I hired you for the summer. If you don't like what I talk about, get back in the truck and drive. You knew what I was like when you made the bet, so don't be trotting out excuses for welshing. And you will welsh, schoolgirl. After three solid weeks of the Rocking M, you'll be champing at the bit to see the bright lights just like the other females who came here."

"West Fork doesn't have any bright lights worth seeing."

"You should have hung around the OK Corral a little longer," Luke said sardonically.

Carla's temper frayed. She hated being reminded

of how many times she had made a fool of herself around Luke.

"Did it ever occur to you it might have been the MacKenzie *men* rather than the Rocking M's isolation, that drove their wives into town?" Carla asked in a sugary voice.

"Don't bet on it. None of the MacKenzie men ever got any complaints in bed. It was being alone in the daytime that got to the women."

Carla set her jaw so hard her teeth ached. The thought of Luke in bed literally took away her breath. Part of it was a virgin's fear of the unknown—but most of her breathlessness came from a very female curiosity about what it would be like to be Luke's lover, to feel his big body moving against hers, to hear his breath quicken at her touch and to taste again the warmth of his own breath.

"Which will it be?" he demanded. "The big house or the road?"

"The house."

No sooner were the words out of her mouth than Carla wondered if history were repeating itself and she was making a bad mistake because Luke's presence always muddled what few wits she had.

Before Carla could take back her words, Luke brushed past her and began unloading the truck.

"You brought enough stuff for the summer," he said, surprised.

"*Quelle* shock," Carla muttered. "The bet was for the summer, wasn't it?"

Luke gave her a sideways glance. "I said you could back out anytime. When I give my word, I keep it."

She took a deep breath and set fire to her last bridge to safety. "And I told you I wouldn't back out as long as I'm treated like any other hand. My word means just as much to me as yours means to you."

He searched her eyes for a long moment before he nodded. "All right, schoolgirl. I'll show you your room."

4

Luke set the last of Carla's baggage just inside the door to the small upstairs suite that would be hers for the summer. Standing on tiptoe, staring over his back, Carla looked at the room and made a small sound of astonishment.

"What incredible furniture! Where did you get that headboard? And the dresser," she added, looking away from the queen-size bed. Without thinking, she crowded against Luke so that she could touch the satin surface of the wood. "The design is perfect, all curves, like running water or granite smoothed by rain. Where on earth did you find—"

"Leave your stuff for now," Luke said, all but pushing Carla out of the room and closing the door behind himself. The last thing he wanted to do was to talk about the furniture he had made three years ago in an effort to exorcise or appease the yearning within himself for the life and the girl he could not have. "I'll show you the kitchen next, then I've got to check on one of the mares."

Carla started to point out that she had seen the kitchen before, then shut her mouth. She had demanded to be treated like any other employee, and that's what Luke was doing. What she hadn't realized was that he would treat her like a stranger as well, refusing to answer even such relatively impersonal questions as where he had found the beautiful bedroom set.

Without a word Carla followed Luke down the stairs. The muscular ease of his walk fascinated her. Her glance lingered on the width of his shoulders beneath his blue work shirt and the powerful lines of his back as it tapered to a worn, wide leather belt encircling a lean waist. His jeans were faded in patterns determined by sun and sweat rather than by commercial acid washes. His boots were scarred by stirrups, spurs and brush.

The stairs ended in a hall whose floor was covered by earth-colored, unglazed Mexican tiles. Mentally Carla noted that a lot of that earth color might come off with a mop and a bucket of soapy water. The kitchen floor was of the same unglazed tiles.

Make that several buckets of soapy water.

With an inaudible sigh Carla noted the abundant signs of months of indifferent house cleaning. Windows were streaked where they weren't smeared. The counters, cupboards, drawers and appliances in the kitchen and adjoining laundry room had the dull shine of grease rather than the subtle shine of cleanliness.

Luke followed Carla's glance to the far corner of the kitchen, where chunks of spring mud still clung to the baseboard even though spring had passed. Tomato sauce or gravy—or both—made an uneven pattern down the bank of drawers to the right of the sink. On the floor, distinct paths crisscrossed from the back door to the sink to the stove and into the big dining room.

"The last four cooks weren't much on housekeeping," Luke muttered.

"Really? I thought it was just your wallpaper."

Luke glanced at the walls and grimaced. They were worse than the floor. He tried to remember the last time the walls had been scrubbed. He couldn't.

"I'll have one of the men wash them down."

"Don't bother, unless you plan to keep eating off them."

Unwillingly, Luke smiled. "It does look sort of like we've been serving dinner off the walls instead of the table, doesn't it?"

"Mmm," was the most tactful thing Carla could think of to say. "Do you want a late or early dinner?"

"Six and six."

"What?"

"Breakfast at six and dinner at six. The men who need a cold lunch packed for them will tell you at dinner the night before. Otherwise just see that the bunkhouse kitchen stays stocked with snacks and sandwich stuff.''

Luke ran a finger lightly over the huge, six-burner gas stove and came up with a greasy fingertip for his trouble. He muttered something and wiped his hand on his jeans.

"What?" asked Carla.

"I've been so busy working on the ranch that I didn't realize the house had gone to hell."

"Nothing a little soap and water won't cure," Carla said with determined cheerfulness.

Or dynamite, she added silently, looking around. When she looked up again, Luke was studying her.

"If any of the hands bother you, let me know," he said.

"I don't mind them coming around and asking me to bake cookies for them," Carla answered, remembering other summers. "I could live without king snakes in the pantry, though."

Luke's lips twitched as he remembered the incident when an ambitious king snake had followed mice into the pantry. The snake had set up housekeeping among the sacks of rice and flour. At least, that was what each and every hand had solemnly sworn when Luke had heard Carla's scream and come running. He had caught the snake and taken it to the barn, where its predatory efforts would be more appreciated. Then he had begun questioning the hands very closely.

The shadow of a smile faded from Luke's mouth.

"I wasn't worried about that kind of snake. It's the two-legged variety I had in mind. If one of my men makes you uncomfortable, let me know."

Carla looked perplexed. "I've never had any trouble with the hands before."

"The last time you spent a summer here, you looked more like a boy than a girl," Luke said bluntly. His gaze went from Carla's gold-streaked chestnut hair to her slender feet and back up again, silently cataloguing each lush curve. "No such luck this time. My men aren't blind. So if anyone crowds you, don't try to take care of it yourself. Come running to me or Ten and come fast. Got that?"

"I don't dress to catch a man's eye," Carla said matter-of-factly, indicating her summer uniform of jeans and one of her brother's old shirts with sleeves rolled up and trailing ends knotted to one side. "There shouldn't be any problem."

Luke's left eyebrow climbed as he followed Carla's gesture. "Maybe. But if you swipe another one of my shirts, I'll take it out of your soft hide."

"This is my brother's shirt," she said indignantly, holding up a black shirttail in her hand.

Luke shook his head. "I got oil on it working on Cash's balky Jeep, so he loaned me a clean one for your birthday party."

"Figures," she muttered. "It's so comfortable I've been tempted to use it as a nightgown. Nylon is too cold or too hot. Your shirt was all soft and perfect."

Abruptly Carla's mouth went dry. The thought that the cloth draped so intimately around her body had once been wrapped just as intimately around Luke's sent an arrow of sensation glittering from her breastbone to the pit of her stomach. She swallowed and looked away from his clear, penetrating eyes.

"Don't worry," she said huskily. "I'll give it back to you as soon as it's washed."

"No hurry. I've still got Cash's shirt."

Silence stretched and then stretched some more, leaving Carla feeling breathless, uncertain. She looked back at Luke, only to find him watching her with unnerving intensity, as though he were measuring precisely where the disputed shirt fit her differently than it fit him.

"How do you want to arrange your time off?" he asked.

"What?"

Slowly Luke lifted his eyes to Carla's face.

"Your time off. Do you want to work six days and have one off, or do you want to work right through, or do you want to save up some days and take a little vacation?"

"I'll save them up," Carla said promptly.

"That's what the women all say at first, but after a few weeks they can't get to West Fork fast enough."

"Cash will be coming up in early August. I'll wait."

Luke's smile told Carla that he didn't believe it.

He turned toward the back door. "If you need anything, holler. I'll be in the barn."

With a mixture of relief and disappointment, Carla watched Luke leave. The relief she understood; the disappointment she ignored. She looked around the kitchen, wondering where to begin. Everywhere she looked, a task cried out to be done. Fortunately she had the ability to organize her time. She didn't always use that ability, but she had it just the same.

"The cleaning will have to wait," Carla muttered, looking at the clock. "In two hours, twelve hungry hands will descend. Thirteen, counting Luke. Call it fourteen. Luke is big enough for two men. Then there's me. Dinner for fifteen, coming right up."

The number she had to feed seemed to echo in the silent kitchen. *Fifteen. My God. No wonder all the pots and pans are so big.*

The thought of feeding that many people was daunting. Carla had never cooked whole meals for more than herself, her brother and, when she was on the ranch, for Luke. The three of them had eaten in the old ranch house, whose small rooms were famous for mice, drafts and dust in equal measure.

Looking around, Carla gave each black sleeve another turn upward to make sure the cloth didn't get in the way. Then she went to the refrigerator and began taking a fast inventory of what was available.

The refrigerator held beer, apple juice, horseradish, ketchup, a chunk of butter, four eggs, a slab of unsliced bacon and an open package of baloney that had quietly curled up and died. The big freezer opposite the stove was more rewarding. It held enough meat, mostly beef, to feed half the state of Colorado. As long as the propane held out, they wouldn't starve. All she had to do was thaw a few roasts in the microwave.

"Oops," Carla said, glancing around. "No microwave. Not enough time to cook frozen roasts, either."

She went to the pantry, hoping for inspiration. "Canned stew, canned chili, canned chicken…yuck. No wonder Luke is short-tempered. Eating out of cans is enough to sour the disposition of a saint." The other side of the pantry was no better. She was confronted by a solid wall of cans as big as buckets—tomatoes, peas, green beans, corn, pitted cherries and coffee. There were also half-empty fifty-pound sacks of flour, sugar, rice, cornmeal and dried apples. The bread bin held four wizened crusts.

"So much for hamburgers," she said unhappily, "and I doubt if anyone delivers pizza this far out."

A burlap bag bulged with potatoes. Another bag was full of onions. Pinto beans dribbled out of a third bag. She grabbed that bag with both hands and lifted. It weighed at least ten pounds. That was enough beans to make real chili or *fríjoles refritos* or any number of dishes. She could feed an army— but not in the next two hours.

Behind the bag of beans Carla spotted a cardboard

box that had been shoved aside and forgotten. Inside the box was package after package of spaghetti. Each package held two pounds of the slender, dried pasta. The fragile sticks had been broken but were perfectly edible otherwise.

"I sense a spaghetti dinner on the horizon," Carla said.

She grabbed two packages, hesitated, and grabbed two more. When she cooked for Cash and herself, a pound of dried pasta fed both of them with enough left over for several of her lunches. But then, she always served fresh salad, garlic bread and dessert with the spaghetti. Bread and salad were out of the question, so she grabbed an extra package of pasta, bringing the total to ten pounds.

"My God, it will take an army to eat this much. I'll be making cold spaghetti sandwiches for weeks and the hands will riot and Luke will tear a strip off me big enough to cover the south pasture."

Carla frowned at the last package of pasta, then decided she could always take the leftovers to the bunkhouse for the hands who wanted a midnight snack. Arms bulging with packages of spaghetti, she went back into the kitchen. There she dumped the pasta on the counter and went back to the freezer. The hamburger came in five-pound freezer packages that were frozen as solid as a stone.

She unwrapped a brick of ground meat and dropped it into a cast-iron frying pan that was so big and heavy it took both hands for her to lift it up onto the stove. A box of wooden matches sat on the stove itself. She lit the burner beneath the frozen meat, covered the pan and went to work on the sauce. Several forays to the pantry resulted in a can of tomato sauce the size of a bathroom sink, an equally intimidating can of whole tomatoes, and ten fat onions.

After rummaging in the cupboards near the stove, Carla found a kettle the size of a laundry tub. She set it aside for cooking the noodles and found a slightly smaller cousin to hold the sauce. She nearly had to turn the kitchen inside out to find a hand-held can opener that worked. As she wrestled with the awkward can and poured a river of tomato sauce into a big pot—too quickly—she discovered how the kitchen walls had gotten their splatter patterns. She wiped up what she could reach, lit the burner under the sauce and went to work peeling and chopping onions. Between bouts of crying she prodded the hamburger, prying off bits of meat as the frozen block slowly loosened.

By the time the hamburger had thawed and was browning with the onions in the huge pan, nearly an hour had passed. A determined search of the kitchen had turned up no oregano and no whole garlic. A geriatric bottle of garlic granules was available, but she had to hammer the plastic container on the counter to knock loose a little of the contents.

"What on earth have the cooks been feeding everyone?" Carla asked in exasperation. "No herbs, no spices, no—'' The clock caught her eye. ''Uh-oh. I'd better get dessert going or there won't be any of that, either.''

Carla ran up to her bedroom suite, tore through four boxes until she found her cookbooks, and raced back downstairs. The recipe for cherry cobbler said it fed eight. She doubled it, spread it into the smallest baking pan she could find—which was half the size of a card table—and discovered that the pan was way too big for the contents.

''Oh well, men always like dessert. I'll put it in their lunch along with the cold spaghetti sandwiches.''

She mixed up two more double batches of cobbler, poured them into the pan with the first batch and lit the oven. Even after doing six times the normal recipe of cobbler, she still had half of the huge can of cherries left over. She set it aside, saw that time was getting away from her and went back to the spaghetti sauce.

The meat and onions were browned and the pot of tomato sauce and chopped tomatoes was finally coming to a boil. The size and weight of the frying pan made draining the meat and onions an awkward process—especially using a kitchen towel as a pot holder—but she finally managed it. Next she had to dump the meat and onions into the pot of sauce. In doing so, she discovered another way to decorate the walls. Muttering, she mopped up and told herself that she would have to learn to manhandle a heavy pot and a gallon or two of sauce without making a mess.

"Speaking of gallons, I'd better get the spaghetti water on," she muttered, pushing back her hair with her elbow because her fingers were only slightly less messy than the walls.

By the time Carla filled a huge pot with water and lugged it to the stove, she finally understood why men rather than women chose careers as chefs; you had to be a weight lifter to handle the kitchen equipment. She turned the fire on high and mopped up the floor where she had spilled water on the way to the stove. The places she left behind were relatively clean, making the rest of the floor look much worse by comparison.

For a moment Carla was tempted to slop a little tomato sauce on the sort-of-clean spots to even things up, thereby delaying the hour of reckoning when she had to clean the floor. She loved to cook but hated housework. She knew her own weakness so well that she worked twice as hard at cleaning, making up for her own dislike of the job.

But it would look really nice with a few dollops of tomato sauce. Nobody would even notice.

Carla managed to avoid the temptation only because she remembered the green beans, which should have been on the stove ten minutes ago. Another trip to the pantry yielded a gallon can of green beans. While they heated, she sliced bacon, fried it and sliced more onions to sauté in the bacon fat. From time to time she checked the spaghetti water.

"I know a watched pot never boils, but this is ridiculous," she said beneath her breath, lifting the lid and testing the water with her fingertip.

Dead cold.

From the barn, corral and bunkhouse came the sounds of men wrapping up tasks in preparation for dinner. Two pickups came in from opposite directions, pulling horse trailers behind. Four men got out and stretched, tired and hungry from a long day of checking cattle on land leased from the federal government. The horses being unloaded from trailers neighed to the horses that were already rubbed down and had begun to tear great mouthfuls of hay from the corral feeding rack.

The men would be just as hungry.

Anxiously Carla listened as the bunkhouse door slammed repeatedly, telling her that the men were going in to wash up for dinner. Laughter and catcalls greeted a cowboy whose jeans showed clear signs of his having landed butt-first in the mud. He gave back as good as he got, reminding the other men of the time one of them had slipped in a fresh cow flop and another had been bucked off into a corral trough.

Carla couldn't help smiling as bits of conversation drifted through the open window. For the first time she realized that she hadn't heard a human voice since Luke had vanished into the barn. The thought went as quickly as it had come, pushed aside by the fact that the spaghetti water was barely lukewarm. At this rate dinner would be at least half an hour late and Luke would be thinking he had gotten the bad end of the bet.

Hurriedly Carla tasted the tomato sauce, added more garlic and checked the spaghetti water again. Nothing doing. The outside door into the dining room squeaked open and then closed. The room, which adjoined the kitchen, was more like a mess hall than a formal dining room. There were two long tables, each of which could seat ten comfortably and fourteen in a pinch, twenty chairs, a wall of floor-to-ceiling cupboards and not much else.

It occurred to Carla that the tables were bare of plates, cups, utensils and napkins, not to mention salt, pepper, ketchup, steak sauce, sugar and all the other condiments beloved by ranch hands. Groaning at her forgetfulness, she dumped the half-cooked on-ions and bacon into the pot of green beans and frantically began opening cupboards, searching for plates. She was so busy that she didn't hear the door between the kitchen and dining room open.

"Smells good in here. What's for supper?"

"Spaghetti," Carla said without turning toward the male voice.

"Smells more like cherry pie."

"Ohmygod, *dessert*."

She raced past the man who had walked into the kitchen. A fast look in the oven assured her that the cobbler had survived her neglect. All she had to do was maneuver the big pan out of the oven to let the cobbler cool. The kitchen towel wouldn't stretch to do the job of handling the pan.

"Pot holders," she muttered, straightening from bending over the oven.

"Looks like cobbler from here."

The voice came from about a foot away from Carla's ear. Her head snapped around and she looked at the man for the first time.

Long, lean and deceptively lazy-looking, Tennessee Blackthorn was watching Carla with an odd smile on his face.

"Ten! Is it really you?" Carla asked, delighted. "The last time I heard, you had a phone call in the middle of the night, went into Cortez and never came back."

"Never is a long time." Smoke-colored eyes swept appreciatively from Carla's oven-flushed cheeks to her ankles and back up. "Guess we can't call you *niña* anymore. You finally grew into those long legs and bedroom eyes."

She laughed. "I love hungry men. They'll flatter the cook shamelessly in hopes of an early dinner. You're out of luck, though. The watched pot isn't boiling."

"He's out of luck, period," Luke said from the back door, his voice cold.

5

Carla didn't realize how much her expression changed when she turned toward Luke, but little escaped Ten's eyes. He measured the complex mixture of yearning and distance, hope and hunger in her look, and he knew that nothing had changed.

"Still chasing moonlight over black water, aren't you?" he asked softly.

If either Carla or Luke heard, neither answered. They were looking at each other as though it had been years, not hours, since their last meeting.

"The pot holders are over there," Luke said in a clipped voice, gesturing toward a drawer near the stove, never looking away from Carla's vivid blue-green eyes.

"Pot holders," Carla repeated, absorbed by the arching line of Luke's eyebrows, the clean curves of his mouth, the shadow of beard lying beneath his tanned skin.

"Pot holders," repeated Luke.

"Still smells and looks like cobbler to me," Ten said to no one in particular.

"Don't you have something to do?" Luke asked pointedly, finally looking away from Carla.

"Nope. But if you give me a cup of coffee I'll find something."

Luke eyed the man who was both his friend and the ramrod of the Rocking M. Ten returned him stare for stare...and smiled. Luke barely controlled his anger. He knew he had no reason to be angry with Ten; of all the ranch hands, the ramrod would be the least likely to hustle Carla into bed. But hearing Ten talk about Carla's *long legs and bedroom eyes* had made Luke savagely angry. The fact that his anger was irrational, and he knew it, only made him more angry.

"Coffee?" Carla asked, feeling a sinking in her stomach. "I forgot to make coffee!"

"How the hell can you forget coffee?" Luke demanded, turning on Carla, glad to find a rational outlet for his anger. "Any ranch cook worth the powder to blow her straight to hell knows that the first thing you make in the morning is coffee and the last thing you clean at night is the coffeepot!"

"Well," drawled Ten, "I guess that sure settles that. Carla isn't a ranch cook and we're going to starve to death opening cans with our pocketknives. Sure you wouldn't like to think it over, boss? Wouldn't want you to go off half-cocked and shoot yourself in the foot."

Luke said something under his breath that made Carla wince. She turned away and began searching through cupboards with hands that shook. All she found was peanut butter, jelly and a jar of pickled jalapeño peppers. She grabbed the jar and shoved it into Luke's hand.

"Here. Suck on one of those. It will cool you off."

Ten's laughter filled the kitchen. Luke slammed the jar back onto the shelf and gave Carla a narrow-eyed look.

"Listen, schoolgirl. This is the real world where men work hard and get hungry. I said dinner at six and I meant it. If you're too immature to get the job done I'll find a woman who can."

Luke turned and left the kitchen before Carla could answer. Not that she had anything to say; she hadn't heard Luke so cold and cutting since the night three years ago when he had told her that she wasn't woman enough to love a man.

"Hey," Ten said gently, "don't take the boss seriously. He's just upset about that black mare of his. She's going downhill fast and the vet can't figure out why."

Carla made a neutral sound and kept on searching the cupboards. She found nothing useful. Part of the problem was that she was fighting against tears. The rest of the problem was that she wanted to throw things.

"Is that big pot boiling yet?" she asked tightly.

Ten lifted the lid. "Nope."

"Close?"

"Nope. I'll tell the men to take their time washing up."

"Thanks."

Carla finally found the pot holders, retrieved the cobbler and set it aside to cool. While looking for the pot holders she also found the coffeepot. Like everything else in the kitchen, the pot was oversize. It quite literally made gallons of coffee at a time. She filled everything, putting in twice the coffee any sane person would have wanted, and thumped the pot onto the stove to perk.

By the time she lit the burner under the coffee, the spaghetti water was showing vague signs of life. With a heartfelt prayer she slammed the lid back in place and resumed searching the cupboards for plates.

"What are you looking for?" Ten asked from the doorway.

"Plates," Carla said despairingly, shutting another cupboard door with more force than necessary.

"They're in the mess hall, along with knives, forks, spoons and all the rest."

She flashed him a grateful smile. "Thanks."

Ten shook his head as Carla rushed past him, all but running. "Slow down, *niña*. The men won't starve if they have to wait a bit for chow."

"Tell Luke."

"All right."

Carla grabbed Ten's arm as he headed through the kitchen toward Luke's office at the other end of the house.

"I was just kidding," she said quickly.

"I wasn't." Ten looked down at Carla's unhappy face and shook his head. "You haven't been here two hours and already you look like somebody rode you hard and put you away wet. Have you tried telling Luke how you feel?"

"The first day on a job is always tough."

Ten made an impatient sound. "That's not what I meant. Have you told Luke that you're in love with him?"

For an instant Carla felt as though the floor had dropped from beneath her feet. She tried to speak. No words came. Red flooded her face.

Ten sighed. "Hell, Carla. There isn't a man on this place who doesn't know it, except maybe Luke. Don't you think it's time you told him?"

Her lips trembled as she thought about a night three years ago. She licked her dry lips and said carefully, "He knows."

Ten said something harsh beneath his breath, took off his hat and raked his fingers through his black hair. After a moment he sighed and said, "It's none of my business, but damn it, I hate seeing anything as gentle as you get hurt. Chasing something that doesn't want to be caught can be real painful."

"That's not..." Carla's voice faded. "That's not why I'm here. I came to cure myself of loving...of my childish infatuation..." She swallowed twice and tried again, holding her voice steady with an effort. "I think Luke must have guessed why I'm here, so he's doing everything he can to help the process along."

It was Ten's turn to be speechless. He shook his head and turned away, swearing softly. As an afterthought he added, "I'll set the table."

"Thank you, Ten. I'll be more together tomorrow, I promise." Silently Carla added, *I've got to be. I can't spend the summer holding my breath, feeling my heart beat like a wild bird in a net, listening, listening, listening for Luke's footsteps, his voice, his laughter.*

The rattle of the lid against the pot of spaghetti water jarred Carla from her unhappy reverie. The water was boiling energetically. She added salt and oil and began ripping apart packages of pasta. By the time the last package went in, the water was back to lying motionless in the pot. Anxiously she looked at the big kitchen clock. Six-twenty.

At least the vegetable part of the meal was ready. It was only canned green beans, but the bacon and onion gave the limp beans a whiff of flavor. Carla would have felt better if she had had a few loaves of garlic bread to put out on the table as well, but there was no help for it. Pasta, meat sauce, green beans and cobbler were all that was available. And she didn't even have that. Not yet.

Worst of all, the coffee water was barely warm.

Stifling a groan, Carla rushed into the dining room and began helping Ten distribute cutlery around the tables, which had been pushed together to make a single large rectangle. The surface of the table itself dismayed her; it was no cleaner than the kitchen counters or walls. Whoever had wiped the table in the past had rearranged rather than removed the grease.

"Wait," Carla said to Ten. "The table needs cleaning."

"You start cleaning now and we won't eat until midnight."

She bit her lip. Ten was right.

"Where does Luke keep the tablecloths?" she asked.

"The what?"

She groaned, then had an inspiration. "Newspapers. Where does Luke keep the old newspapers?"

"In the wood box in the living room."

A few minutes later Carla ran back to the dining room carrying a three-inch stack of newspapers. Soon the big table was covered by old news and advertisements for cattle feed and quarter-horse stud service. By the time she and Ten had finished laying out silverware, the hands were beginning to mill hopefully in the yard beyond the dining room. One of the braver men—an old hand called Cosy—stuck his head in the back door. Before he could open his mouth, Ten started talking."

"I said I'd call when chow was on." The ramrod's cold gray eyes measured Cosy. "You getting hard of hearing or are you just senile?"

"No sir," Cosy said, backing out hastily. "I'm just fine. Planning on staying that way, too."

Ten grunted. Cosy vanished. The door thumped shut behind him.

"They must be starving," Carla said, looking as guilty as she felt.

"Nope. They still remember the cookies you used to bake. When Luke told the men you'd be cooking for a few days, they started drooling."

"Tell them to relax. I'll be here all summer, not just for a few days."

Ten shrugged. "The last woman who stayed here more than three weeks was ugly as a rotten stump and drank to boot, but what really got her sent down the road was that she couldn't cook worth a fart in a windstorm."

Carla fought not to smile. She failed.

The left corner of Ten's mouth turned up. "Finally we took up a collection to buy her a bus ticket to Nome."

"Alaska?" asked Carla.

"Yeah. She got a job scaring grizzlies away from salmon nets."

Feminine laughter bubbled up. Soon Ten was laughing, too. Neither one of them noticed the big man who had come to the kitchen through the living room and was now leaning against the corner counter, his thumbs hooked in his belt and his mouth a bleak downward curve. He glanced at the clock. Six-forty. He glanced at the stove. Everything looked hot and ready to go. Whiskey-colored eyes cut back to the laughing couple in the dining room.

Just when Luke had opened his mouth to say something savage on the subject of cooks who couldn't get dinner ready on time, Carla grabbed Ten's wrist and looked at his watch.

"The pasta should be done by now, if the hands don't mind it al dente."

"What?"

"Chewy," she said succinctly.

"Hell, after a day on the range, we'll eat whatever we can get, any way we can get it, including raw."

Carla grimaced. "Yuck. Pasta sticks to your teeth that way."

Laughing, shaking his head, Ten leaned forward and tugged gently on a shining strand of Carla's hair. "I'm glad you're back. You bring sunlight with you."

Almost shyly, Carla said, "Thanks, Ten. It's good to be back. I love this place."

"The place or the owner?"

The question was so soft that Carla could pretend not to have heard it at all. So she smiled at Ten and turned toward the kitchen without answering, not knowing how much her sad smile revealed of her thoughts. As soon as she was through the door she spotted Luke leaning against the counter, impatience and anger in every hard line of his body.

"I was wondering when you'd remember that you were hired to cook, not to flirt with my ramrod."

"I wasn't flir—"

"Like hell you weren't," Luke said curtly, interrupting Carla. "Watch it, schoolgirl. Ten smiles and is handsome as sin, but that soft-drawling SOB has broken more hearts than any twelve men I know. He's not the marrying kind, but he's plenty human. If you throw yourself at him hard enough, he might just reach out and grab what's being offered. And we both know how good you are at throwing yourself."

Carla went pale and turned away.

Luke swore harshly beneath his breath, furious with her and Ten and himself and everything else that came to mind. He watched with narrowed, glittering eyes while Carla grabbed two pot holders and went to the kitchen range. By the time he realized that she was reaching for the wildly boiling kettle of spaghetti and water, it was too late. She was already struggling with the huge kettle, her whole body straining as she lifted at arm's length the weight of five gallons of water and ten pounds of pasta.

Just as Carla realized that she couldn't handle the kettle—and hadn't the strength to lower it without splashing boiling water down her front—Luke's arms shot around her body. He covered her hands with his own and lifted, taking the weight of the kettle from her quivering arms. Together they gently set the heavy pot on the back burner once more. For a few moments neither one moved, shaken by the realization of how close Carla had come to a painful accident.

Luke bent his head, brushing his cheek so lightly against Carla's hair that she couldn't feel it. When he took a breath he smelled flowers. The scent was dizzying, for it carried with it a promise of womanly warmth, a promise that was repeated in Carla's curving hips pressed against his body. She was trembling, breathing with soft, tearing sounds.

Desire turned like an unsheathed knife in Luke's guts, hardening him with shocking speed. He lifted his hands and stepped back as though he had been burned. And he had, but by something hotter than boiling water.

"My God, schoolgirl!" Luke exploded. "Don't you know better than to try to lift five gallons of boiling water off the back of this stove?"

Carla shook her head and said nothing. Nor did she turn around.

"Are you all right?" Luke demanded.

Slowly she nodded.

The line of her neck and shoulders tugged at Luke's emotions, reminding him of how vulnerable she was, how close she had come to hurting herself. The thought of boiling water scoring her soft skin made him feel as though he himself had been burned.

"Sunshine?" Luke said softly. "Are you sure you didn't burn yourself?"

The unexpected gentleness made tears burn beneath Carla's eyelids. She blinked fiercely, not wanting to cry in front of Luke, who already thought her a child. *Schoolgirl.*

"I'm fine," she said, her voice husky.

Carla took a steadying breath and inhaled the scent of Luke, a compound of leather and male heat and the clean fragrance of soap. She longed to turn and put her arms around him, to feel his arms around her, to hold and be held and never let go.

But she hadn't come to the Rocking M for that. She had come to let go of something she had never held.

"Thank you for saving dinner," Carla said, closing her eyes, trying not to breathe, for with each inhalation she took in the warmth and male scent of Luke.

"Dinner?" he asked.

"The spaghetti."

Gently Luke turned Carla around and brought her chin up until he could see her eyes. His breath came in hard, bringing with it the promise of flowers and warmth.

"You could have dumped that spaghetti all over the floor and I wouldn't have given a damn, so long as you weren't burned."

He examined her face intently, then unclenched her fingers and examined them for damage. Gently he traced the backs of her hands and arms until he reached the barrier of rolled-up black sleeves. His sleeves, his shirt, her wide blue-green eyes watching him. He traced her smooth, fine-grained skin one more time and felt desire roll through him like thunder through a narrow canyon, a force that made even stone tremble. He dropped her hands and turned away abruptly.

"Not a mark. You were lucky, schoolgirl. Next time you better think before you grab something too big for you. I might not be around to bail you out."

The change in Luke from tender to abrupt was disorienting to Carla. Before she could stop herself, she said, "I'm not a schoolgirl."

"Last time I checked, the University of Colorado was a school. What do you want me to do with that damned kettle?"

There were several tempting options, but Carla limited herself to the most practical one.

"Pour off the water in the sink."

Luke handled the heavy, awkward kettle with an ease that made Carla flatly envious.

"Now I know why cavewomen put up with cavemen," she muttered to herself, thinking Luke couldn't hear.

But he could. He glanced over his shoulder, saw the compound of admiration and desire in Carla's eyes as she watched him, and didn't know whether to smile or swear at the renewed leap of his blood. As he poured gallons of steaming water into the sink, he couldn't decide whether having Carla around for the summer was the worst idea he had ever had—or the best.

By the time Carla had the spaghetti loaded into a serving dish, the ranch hands were seated around the table in hushed expectancy. As she carried the fragrant, steaming mound of pasta into the dining room, she felt like a lion tamer carrying a single lamb chop into a cage full of big, hungry cats.

"Start a this round," she said. "I'll be back with the sauce in a minute."

The pot with the sauce in it wasn't as awkward as the kettle of boiling water had been, but Luke had taken care of the job anyway. The sauce was now in a soup tureen. A ladle that was twenty inches long stuck out of the rich red sauce.

"Thank you," Carla said, smiling briefly at Luke as she grabbed the tureen. "Go sit down and eat. I can handle the rest."

Without a word Luke lifted the big tureen from Carla's hands and walked into the dining room. She found a big crockery bowl and filled it with green beans. She hurried out to the men.

"Here you are. All I have to do is find a spoon."

An assortment of mumbles greeted her. She didn't hear. She stood rooted to the floor, staring in horrified fascination as the spaghetti bowl made the rounds of the table. Each man heaped his plate with pasta, piling it high and wide, cramming aboard every bit possible and then some. By the time each man had been served, not so much as a single limp strand was left in the huge bowl.

Cosy, who had been the last to be served, took the green beans from Carla and gave her the empty pasta bowl in return.

"If you hurry back with more, you may be able to have a bite yourself before we dig in for seconds," Cosy said, grinning.

The hands who had already buried their pasta in sauce and had begun eating paused long enough to chorus Cosy's remarks. A lot of compliments for her cooking were thrown in, as well.

Carla smiled and tried to acknowledge the praise, but her heart wasn't in it. She was thinking desperately of the gallons and gallons of boiling water that had just gone down the kitchen drain. It would be impossible to cook more spaghetti in time to get it on the table for a second serving. And even if it were possible, at the rate the sauce was disappearing, there wouldn't be anything to put on the pasta but salt, pepper and a splash of ketchup.

Maybe Cosy's just teasing me. Surely no man could eat one of those huge servings and come back for more.

Carla looked toward Ten, who had been the first man to be served. He was better than halfway through his plate and showed not one sign of slowing down.

My God. Even Cash doesn't eat that much, except

*when we're camping and he's been tramping all
over getting rock samples.*

Realization hit. A day's work out on the open
range was certainly the equivalent of Cash's geological explorations. The hands were definitely going to be coming back for seconds.

The bowl of green beans thumped onto the table.
Carla turned and headed back for the kitchen.

"Aren't you going to eat?" Luke asked as he
reached for the rapidly vanishing sauce.

"I'm not hungry."

Carla hurried into the kitchen and began opening
can after can of chili.

6

The memory of that first night as the Rocking M's cook still had the power to raise color in Carla's cheeks a month later. The ranch hands had ribbed her mercilessly but not unkindly; Luke had muttered something about cooking for men instead of school-boys; and Ten had gotten his head handed to him for pointing out that the food was four times as good as anything they had eaten in years, so why complain over short rations?

In fact, Ten had gotten his head handed to him on a regular basis since Carla had come to the ranch. From the look on Luke's face at the moment, Ten was about to get another full serving of his boss's temper. Hurriedly Carla tried to take the scrub brush from Ten's hand.

"Thanks for the help, but Luke is right. He didn't hire you to clean walls."

"You've been working longer hours than any hand since you got here," Ten said calmly, hanging on to the brush. "This is my day off, and if I want to scrub kitchen walls, I'll damned well scrub kitchen walls."

Luke looked at Carla's drawn, unhappy face and felt his temper rise even higher. Ten was right; Carla had been working twelve-hour days since she had come to the ranch. Every floor in the ranch house was clean enough to eat from. The kitchen counters and cupboards gleamed with cleanliness, as did the beaten-up wooden tables in the dining room. Thanks to Carla's detailed shopping lists, the pantry and cupboards were packed with various foods, the refrigerator was bursting with fresh fruits and vegetables, and a menu was posted in the dining room so that the men would know just what the coming week held in the way of meals.

Even as Luke stood glaring at Ten and Carla, the kitchen was fragrant with the smell of chocolate chip cookies baking in the range's huge oven. Apple, cherry and blueberry pies had become staple items at the dinner table. Homemade baking powder biscuits and bread helped to fill in the cracks. Waffles and pancakes were common breakfast fare. Fresh brownies appeared in lunch bags with gratifying regularity.

And Carla looked as though she hadn't eaten a bit of any of the bounty. Luke suspected she had lost weight since she had come to the ranch. He was certain that she smiled less frequently than ever in his memory. He was also certain that he was the cause of her unhappiness. Each time he told himself that he wouldn't lose his temper with her again, he would see her looking up at Ten with wide eyes and laughter trembling on her lips; and then Luke would feel anger racing through his blood, driving out the desire that was so much a part of him these days that he barely noticed it.

Luke tried to tell himself he was grateful that Carla no longer followed him around like a lost puppy, but he didn't believe it. Slowly, painfully, he had come to the realization that he had wanted Carla at the ranch for the summer because of her transparent feelings for him, not despite them.

For the past four weeks he had thought often of other summers when he had been the sun in her sky…and she had been the sun in his. At some deep, hidden level of his mind, he had wanted to know again that feeling of being special to someone. It was a heady sensation, one he had never before known, for his father had been too busy working the ranch to pay much attention to his son; and his mother had had nothing left over from fighting her own interior devils.

Damn it all to hell, Luke fumed silently. *Why did Carla have to grow up and spoil everything?*

There was no answer for Luke's angry question, unless the insistent beat of his own blood was a kind of answer. Maybe Carla hadn't spoiled anything after all. Maybe she had grown up enough not to run away in fear if he held her against his rigid, hungry body and tasted the honey of her mouth once more.

Not a chance. She's just a schoolgirl.

She's twenty-one. A lot of women have kids by the time they're that age—and they didn't get them by running away from a man's kiss, either.

Luke knew his reasoning was true as far as it went. But there was another truth, one that came a lot closer to home, a truth that lay beneath Luke's hair-trigger temper.

There are two men I call friends. She's the kid sister of one of those men.

Yeah. And she's going to break her heart on the other one if I don't stop it.

That's Ten's problem. And Cash's.

But it wasn't, and Luke knew it. He wanted Carla. He wanted to take the clothes from her body and look at her, touch her, taste her, sheathe himself in her until there was nothing but her passionate heat bathing him and ecstasy bursting through both of them. He wanted that until he woke up sweating, shaking, wild.

She is Cash's sister, for God's sake! Have you forgotten that?

No. That's why I waited until she turned twenty-one, old enough to do whatever she damn well pleases.

Silent questions, answers, questions, retorts, questions; and finally the question that had no answer but silence and rage.

Are you going to ask her to marry you?

It was an impossible situation. Luke had vowed long ago that he would never ask a woman to be his wife unless she were ranch-born and ranch-raised, able to accept the hard work and isolation that was a part and parcel of the Rocking M's rugged life.

But Luke had found no ranch girl who could reach down past his harsh exterior and touch his soul. He had found no ranch girl who could make his body leap into readiness with a look, a smile, the clean scent of her skin. That was what Carla did. She made the raw lighting of desire run like liquid fire in his veins.

Gradually Luke realized that Carla was watching him with shadowed, unhappy eyes; and Ten was watching everything with an infuriating smile on his handsome face.

"Counting to a hundred, boss man?" Ten asked in mock sympathy. "You know, you never did have the temper of a saint or a martyr, but lately you could have taught Satan himself a trick or two."

Ten's drawl was as mocking as his smile. Luke felt his hold on his temper slipping. The only thing that made him hang on to his self-control was the certainty that Ten wanted him to lose it.

"Keep pushing, Tennessee. You'll get there."

"I'll take that as a promise."

"Carla, why don't you go check on those kittens in the barn," Luke said, never looking away from

Ten's calm, handsome face. "Make sure none of them get lost."

"The cookies will—"

"I'll take care of them," Luke interrupted, his voice soft. Too soft.

Carla looked from one man to the other with wide, worried eyes. She started to speak, only to have her mouth go dry when Luke looked at her. Without another word she turned away. The taut silence was broken by the light sound of Carla's retreating footsteps. The back screen door squeaked open and banged shut.

Luke waited for a long count of fifteen before he spoke.

"All right, Ten. Let's have it."

"You do know how to tempt a man," muttered Ten, watching Luke with narrow gray eyes.

"So do you. Why are you trying to pick a fight with me?"

Ten didn't bother to deny it. "Just thought I'd give you something as mean as yourself to take out your temper on."

"Meaning?"

"You've been riding Carla hard since she got here. No matter what she does, you tear a strip off her."

"Maybe. And maybe I think my cook has better things to do than chase my ramrod."

"Yeah, I kind of thought that might be the burr under your saddle." Ten's mocking smile faded.

"You don't have a kind word to say to Carla, yet when someone else does, you jump real salty. You never used to be a dog in the manger, but the way you're acting lately, a man might think if you can't have Carla you don't want anyone to have her."

"She's too young to talk about having."

"Bull, boss man. She's a woman all the way to the soles of her feet." Ten saw the shift in Luke's expression, the flash of hunger and anger. The ramrod nodded, satisfied with what he saw. "She's fully of age. If she wants a man, she's entitled."

"Leave her alone, Ten."

"Why? You've made it real clear you don't want her. Hell, it's not like she was a kid anymore. The men in Boulder aren't blind. By now, one of them has probably taught her why women are soft and men are hard."

"Drop it."

Ten sighed, lifted his hat and raked his fingers through his black hair. "You're being a damned fool," he said calmly. "The way I see it, Carla has loved you for years and you've pushed her away for years. Finally you made it stick. She went off to college and found men who didn't push her away. She grew up. Then she came back to see how you stacked up against her memories and her new experiences with men."

"Carla isn't the type to sleep around," Luke said tightly.

"Who said anything about sleeping around?"

Ten retorted. "I was talking about a young girl who was sent out of here with her pride in shreds. Seems to me she could be forgiven for finding a nice boy or two who wanted to kiss all the wounds and make her feel like a woman instead of a 'schoolgirl.'"

Luke said not one word, but the thought of Carla being touched by another man shook him. The thought of her being taken by anyone sent a killing rage through Luke's veins. He had been so sure, so unspeakably certain, that she would never allow anyone to touch her but him.

Ten measured the barely contained rage in Luke's expression and shrugged. "Suit yourself, boss man. But you should know one thing. Carla told me she came here this summer to get over you. You keep riding roughshod over her feelings and she'll walk out of here at the end of the summer and never look back. Then where will you be? You may not be her first man, but so what? You're the one who was given first call and you turned her down flat. Your fault, not hers. You'll never find another woman with half what she has to offer and you know it."

There was a long, taut silence while Luke measured Ten with the cold yellow eyes of a cornered mountain lion.

"I wasn't cut out to live in a city," Luke said finally.

"Did she ask you to?"

"No, but sooner or later she would. The Rocking M is hell on women. I'd rather not marry at all than have a woman walk out on her kids and her husband, or hit the bottle or go crazy staying on the ranch and make everyone's life a living hell.''

"Carla wouldn't—"

"Like flaming hell she wouldn't," Luke said savagely. "Do you think my mother or my aunts *wanted* to betray their children and husbands? Do you think my father or my uncles deliberately picked weak women to marry? Do you think I want to watch Carla get thin and sullen grieving for a way of life she can't have if she's my wife? Or maybe you think I should be like some college kid and just take what she's offering and not worry about marriage, is that it?"

Ten swore beneath his breath, the words all the more violent for the softness of his voice.

"Now you're beginning to understand," Luke said. "Stay away from her, Ten. This is the only warning you'll get."

"What if I'm thinking of marriage?"

Luke closed his eyes for an instant. When they opened there was no emotion showing; not anger, not fear, not desire, nothing but an icy emptiness.

"Are you thinking of marriage?" he asked softly.

"She's the kind of woman that makes a man think of hearth fires and long winter nights and babies teething on your knuckles," Ten said. Then he sighed, raked his fingers through his hair again and added, "But that's all it will ever be for this cowboy. Thinking. Dreaming. I'm piss-poor husband material and no one knows it better than I do." He jerked his hat into place and met Luke's eyes. "Ease off on the spurs, Luke. Carla has a real tender hide where you're concerned."

"And if I don't?" Luke asked, more curious than angry.

"I'll get to feeling protective and you'll jump salty one too many times and we'll have hell's own fight. Then you'll be short one ramrod and the ranch will be short one boss." Ten smiled wolfishly. "You're bigger than I am, but you'd start out fighting fair. I wouldn't. Be quite a brawl while it lasted."

Unwillingly Luke smiled in return, then laughed. After a moment his face settled into grim lines once more.

"Hell of a mess, isn't it?" Luke said quietly.

"It'll do," agreed Ten. "Why in God's name did you let Carla come to the ranch this summer if you knew it was going to drive you crazy?"

"I..." Luke closed his eyes and shook his head. "It seemed like a good idea at the time. She didn't have a summer job. The Rocking M didn't have a cook. The men were going to rebel if they had to keep eating slop that hogs wouldn't touch. Carla is a fine cook. Some of the best meals I ever had were ones she fixed for Cash and me over in the old house." Luke rubbed the back of his neck and grimaced. "Like I said. It seemed like a good idea at the time. Besides, I expected her to cry uncle by now.''

''Carla?''

''It's been four weeks. She must be dying to see a movie or get her hair fixed or whatever it is that women do in town. I promised her before she ever came back here that all she had to do was say the word and the bet was off, no hard feelings and no regrets.''

''You don't know her very well, do you?.

It was an observation, not a question, but Luke answered anyway.

''What do you mean?''

''Carla never backed up an inch for anyone, including that hardheaded brother of hers. She made a deal with you. She'll keep it or die trying.'' Realization hit Ten. ''That's why you're riding her so hard—you think you can goad her into quitting.''

Luke looked uncomfortable but said nothing.

''Not one chance in hell, buddy,'' Ten said succinctly. ''Carla may be pretty to look at and have a smile as soft as a rose petal, but that's one determined girl. Think about that the next time you start in on her. You're beating a hog-tied pony. She can't escape.''

Luke's breath came in harshly. He hadn't thought about Carla in that way, as a person of pride and determination. He had seen her either as a girl too young for him or as one more woman who would be ground up by the Rocking M's isolation and demands. His breath hissed out in an explosive curse.

Ten smiled sympathetically. ''You've got your tail in a real tight crack. It's pretty hard on a man when he's damned if he does and damned if he doesn't.''

''Do us both a favor, Ten,'' Luke said, giving the other man a hard look.

''Sure.''

''Stop trying to run interference for Carla. Every time you start hovering over her like a mother hen, I get to thinking about how good stewed chicken would taste.''

There was an instant's silence before Ten threw back his head and laughed. He was still laughing when Luke set out for the barn with angry, long-legged strides.

7

"Did you find that ghost stud yet?" Ten asked Luke.

The ramrod's voice had no inflection but his smoke-gray eyes were lit with a combination of sympathy and laughter. Ten knew that Luke had spent long hours out on the range in order to avoid being close to Carla, not to find the near-mythical black stallion that inhabited the narrow red canyons and rugged breaks of the extreme southeastern portion of the Rocking M.

"No, but I saw his tracks a time or two," Luke retorted, piling a huge helping of roast beef, browned potatoes and gravy on his plate.

He glanced up as Carla put a bowl of crisp, fresh green beans next to his plate. With difficulty he forced himself to watch his dinner instead of Carla. She was more beautiful to him each time he looked at her. The thought that he had driven her into the arms of some college boy had tormented Luke. His days had become longer and longer, but even half-dead from overwork, he had only to look at Carla to feel hot claws of desire sinking into him.

Finally Luke's thoughts had driven him to stay away from the ranch house entirely. He had spent five days roaming the Rocking M, sleeping out, waking with his whole body hot, clenched, burning with passion. During the day he had chased his thoughts as though they were cloud shadows flying over the face of the land.

At the end of five days, Luke still hadn't decided which was worse, the thought that Carla had had another man, or the realization that her virginity would no longer be a barrier holding them apart. They wanted each other. They were both of age. They could take each other, work the passion out of their systems, and then they could go on with life the only way that made any sense.

Separately.

She came here to cure herself of me. Why the hell hold back? Why not take what we both want so bad that we can't look at each other without shaking?

"Thanks," Luke said to Carla, his voice harsher than he had meant it to be.

Carla's smile was soft and hesitant, for Luke's expression was forbidding. He had been out on the range for the past five days; even before that he had been distant. Ever since he and Ten had argued almost four weeks ago. If they had argued. Ten had refused to talk about it. In any case, there certainly seemed to be no anger between the two men now.

For a few unguarded moments, Carla's luminous blue-green eyes watched Luke with transparent hunger, measuring the changes five days had made. His beard stubble had become a thick darkness from cheek to jaw, making his rare smiles flash by comparison. He looked tired, drawn, as though he had been sleeping as badly as she had.

Forcing herself not to linger at the table with Luke, Carla went back to the kitchen. She had already done the dinner dishes and was in the process of mixing up a quadruple batch of cookies. No matter how many cookies she made, they disappeared in a matter of hours. There were times when she thought the men were feeding them to the cows.

"Got any more of that coffee?" called Luke from the dining room.

"About a gallon. How's the gravy holding out?"

"You could bring a quart of that, too."

Carla smiled to herself as she filled another gravy boat, grabbed two hot pads and wrapped them around the thin wire handle of the coffeepot. When she got to the dining room, Ten was gone.

"Where's Ten?"

Luke grimaced at Carla's mention of the other man. "In the bunkhouse, I imagine. Why? You need something?"

"No. I was just wondering how Cosy's hand is doing."

Luke took the gravy boat and began drowning potatoes. "What did Cosy do this time?"

"He cut himself and wouldn't go to the doctor. I sewed it up as best I could, but I'm no surgeon."

Gravy slopped heavily from the boat and ran down onto the clean table as Luke's head snapped toward Carla.

"You *what*?" he asked.

"I sewed Cosy up with the curved needle and silk thread I have in my camping kit. Cash taught me how to do it years ago. He's forever cutting his hands when he's out prospecting. Most of the time a butterfly bandage will get the job done, but Cosy wouldn't hear of anything that fancy. He said a plain old needle and thread was all he wanted. When I was finished he doused everything in the gentian violet solution I've been putting on the calf that cut itself on wire." She glanced aside at Luke's plate. "Your gravy is getting away."

Luke looked down, scooped up runaway gravy on his finger and licked it off. He had to repeat the process several times before the problem was taken care of. At the same time he watched Carla while she set down the coffeepot, shifted the hot pads so that both hands were protected and poured him a mug of coffee. She maneuvered the awkward pot with unexpected grace. Nearly two months of working on the ranch had taught her how to handle the heavy kitchen equipment.

"You do that real slick," Luke said.

Carla looked up, startled. "What?"

For a moment Luke forgot what he had been saying. Carla's eyes were close, clear, like blue-green river pools lit from within. Her lips were full and pink, their soft curves a silent invitation to a man's hungry mouth.

"The coffeepot," Luke said, his voice deep. "You handle it like you've been doing it all your life."

"Pain is a great teacher," Carla said dryly. "You don't have to get burned more than two or three times before you figure out that there's no future in hurting."

Luke's eyes narrowed to glittering amber slits as her words sliced through him like razors. *Pain is a great teacher. There's no future in hurting.* He wondered if Ten had been right, if Carla had come back to the Rocking M to cure herself of the pain of wanting a man who didn't want her.

But Luke did want her. He wanted her until he welcomed pain as a diversion from the agony gnawing in his guts whenever he looked at her and saw what he should not have. Even if she weren't innocent, she was still his best friend's kid sister; and even if she had been a complete stranger, there was still the grim truth about the Rocking M and women. The two didn't mix, as every MacKenzie man but one had found to his grief.

And yet there Carla stood, watching Luke with hungry, haunted, haunting eyes, making his body harden in a single wild rush, forcing him to bite back a curse and a groan.

Stop looking at me, he railed at Carla silently. *Stop wanting me. Can't you feel what you're doing to me? Is this revenge for what I did to you three years ago?*

The words went no farther than Luke's mind, for he had just discovered that the protective layer of anger he had wrapped around himself since Carla had arrived was gone, worn out by nearly eight weeks of use. Nothing came to him in his need except a bone-deep weariness and the understanding that Ten had been half-right—Luke had been beating a hog-tied pony.

But the pony was himself, not Carla.

Wearily Luke rubbed his neck with his right hand, trying to loosen his muscles. It wasn't the endless days of hard driving and hard riding that had tied him in knots; it was that he had run and run and run—and then looked up only to find himself in the same place where he had started, reflected in the eyes of Cash's kid sister.

"Did the big storm catch you on the wrong side of Picture Wash?"

Carla's soft question sank slowly into Luke's churning thoughts. All that hadn't been said sank in, as well—her hesitation even to speak to him, her concern that he had been out in the open when thunder rolled down from the peaks and the earth shuddered, and her yearning simply to hear his voice answering her own.

Luke knew just how painful that yearning was, for he had been haunted in exactly the same way. He had heard Carla's voice on the wind, in the darkness, in the silver veils of rain sliding over ancient cliffs. More than once he had awakened in the night, certain that he had only to reach out to feel her softness and warmth curled alongside his body; but his seeking hands had found only darkness and the cold, rust-colored earth of the remote canyon where he had camped.

"No," Luke said softly. "I was back in one of those side canyons where the cliffs make an overhang that keeps out the rain."

"Like September Canyon?"

"Yes. Did Cash tell you about that place?"

"No. You did, when I was fourteen and you gave me a fragment of Anasazi pottery you had found along September Creek. I still have the shard. It's my...talisman, I guess. It reminds me of all that once was and all that might yet be."

Carla looked past Luke and the ranch house walls, seeing the canyon whose existence had haunted her almost as much as Luke. Both the canyon and the man were aloof, distant, compelling. Both of them fascinated her.

Luke's breath came in and stayed, for there was such yearning in Carla's voice and face that it made his throat close.

"Cash promised to take me to September Canyon when he comes in August," she continued. "I'll taste the rain winds and hear water rushing over stone, and I'll see in every shadow a culture that was old before Columbus set sail for India and found the New World."

"I never found any ruins," Luke said finally. "I know they're there, probably way up September Creek or Picture Wash or maybe even Black Springs..." His eyes took on a faraway look in the moments before he shrugged and returned to eating. "The ranch takes too much time for me to have much left over for chasing legends."

"I'm surprised Cash hasn't found any Indian ruins. He must have crawled over every square inch of the Rocking M."

Luke shook his head. "Not a chance. There are parts of this ranch that no one has ever walked, white or Indian. Besides, Cash has been poking around hard rock country. He's a granite and quartz man. Most ruins are found way up washes or creeks that wind between sandstone walls. No gold to be found there. Beautiful country, though. Wild as an eagle and damned near as hard to get to."

"The Anasazi and their natural fortresses..." Carla focused on Luke with intense, blue-green eyes, grateful to have found a neutral subject that interested both of them. "Have you ever wondered what frightened the Anasazi so much that they withdrew to those isolated canyons?"

"Other men, what else? You don't go to all the trouble of building your towns halfway up the face of a sheer cliff, risking the life of every man, woman, and child as they climb up and down to tend the crops or draw water, for any animal less dangerous than man."

"In the end running and hiding didn't do the Anasazi any good. The ruins remain. The people are long gone."

"Maybe," Luke said softly. "And maybe it's like mourning the passing of the Celts. They didn't die so much as they became something else. I think some of the Anasazi came down out of their fortresses and changed into something else. I'll bet Anasazi blood flows in Ute and Apache, Navaho and Zuni and Hopi. Especially the Hopi."

Carla looked at Luke curiously. "You sound like you've studied the Anasazi."

"Self-defense." He looked up at her and grinned. "You asked me so many questions after I gave you that piece of pottery, I had to dig pretty deep for answers. Cash must have mailed me most of the university library."

She laughed, then shook her head. "Poor Luke. I must have pestered you half to death. You were incredibly patient with me."

"I didn't mind the questions. When it was too dark or wet or frozen to work, I'd sit and thumb through those books, looking for answers and finding more questions than even you had."

Luke's long fingers caressed his coffee cup absently as he remembered the long, quiet evenings. Carla watched his hand with unconscious longing.

"When the snow piled up in the canyons," he continued, "I'd sit and think about people who lived and died speaking a language I've never heard and never will, worshipping unknown gods, building stone fortresses with such care that no mortar was needed, block after block of raw stone resting seamlessly next to its mates. However else the Anasazi succeeded or failed as a people, they were craftsmen of the kind this earth seldom sees. That's a good thing to be remembered by."

Luke lifted his coffee cup in a silent salute to Carla. "So you see, your curiosity about that little piece of pottery I gave you opened up a whole new piece of history for me. I call it a fair trade."

"More than fair," she said, her voice husky with memories. "You gave me a world at the very time my own had been jerked out from under my feet."

Luke frowned, remembering the unhappy, fragile fourteen-year-old whose eyes had held more darkness than light. Not for the first time, he cursed the fate that took from a girl her mother and her father in one single instant along an icy mountain road.

"Cash gave you the world," Luke said quietly. "I just sort of came along for the ride."

Carla shook her head slowly but said nothing. She had already embarrassed herself once telling Luke of her love for him; there was no need to repeat the painful lesson. She had been only fourteen when she had looked into his tawny eyes and had seen her future.

It had taken her seven years to realize that she hadn't seen his future, as well.

"Sit down and have some coffee," Luke said. "You look...tired."

Carla hesitated, then smiled. "All right. I'd like that. I'll get a mug."

"We can share mine," he said carelessly. "I'll even put up with cream and sugar, if you like."

"No need. I taught myself to like coffee black."

What Carla didn't say was that she had learned to like black coffee because that was the way Luke drank it. Even after the disaster three years before, she had sat in her college apartment sipping the bitter brew and pretending Luke was sitting across from her, drinking coffee and talking about the Rocking M, the mountains and the men, the cottonwood-lined washes and stands of piñon and juniper, and the sleek, stubborn cattle.

When Carla put her hand on the back of a chair that was several seats away from Luke's, he stood and pulled out the chair next to his. After only an instant of hesitation, she went and sat in the chair he had chosen for her.

"Thank you," she said in a low voice.

Behind Carla, Luke's nostrils flared as he once again drank in the scent of her, flowers and warmth and elemental promises she shouldn't keep. Not with him.

Yet he wanted her the way he wanted life itself, and he had no more anger with which to keep her at bay. He had only the truth, more bitter than the blackest coffee. With a downward curl to his mouth, he poured more of the black brew into his mug and handed it to her.

"Settle in, sunshine. I think it's time you learned the history of the Rocking M."

8

"This land wasn't settled as fast as the flatlands of Texas or the High Plains of Wyoming," Luke said. "Too much of the Four Corners country stands on end. Hard on men, harder on cattle and hell on women. The Indians were no bargain, either. The Navaho were peaceable enough, but roving Ute bands kept things real lively for whites and other Indians. It wasn't until Black Hawk was finished off after the Civil War that whites came here to stay, and most of them weren't what you would call fine, upstanding citizens."

Carla smiled over the rim of the coffee mug. "Didn't the Outlaw Trail run through here?"

"Close enough," admitted Luke. "One of my great-great-greats supposedly was riding through at a hell of a pace, saw the land, liked it and came back as soon as he shook off the folks who were following him."

"Folks? As in posse?"

"Depends on who you talk to. If you talk to the MacKenzie wing of the family, they say Case MacKenzie was just trying to return that gold to its rightful owner. If you talk to other folks, they swear that Case MacKenzie was the one who cleaned out a bank and hit the trail with sixty pounds of gold in his saddlebags, a full-blooded Virginia horse under him and a posse red hot on his trail.

"Who do you believe?"

"Well, I leaned toward the outlaw theory until I showed your brother the MacKenzie gold."

"You still have it?"

"About a handful. Enough that Cash could see right away that it wasn't placer gold. He went back and checked old newspapers. Seems the bank had been taking deposits from the Hard Luck, Shin Splint and Moss Creek strikes. Placer gold, all of it. Smoothed off by water into nuggets or ground down to dust in granite streambeds. The gold my ancestor carried was sharp, bright, running through quartz like sunlight through springwater. Your brother took one look at it and started hunting for Mad Jack's mine."

"Cash never told me about that."

"I asked him not to tell anyone, even you. Last thing I need is a bunch of weekend warriors digging holes in my land."

"You're serious, aren't you? The gold you have really came from Mad Jack's mythical mine?"

"The mine might or might not be myth," Luke

said dryly. "The gold was real, and so was old Mad Jack Turner."

"What makes Cash think the gold came from your ranch?"

"The gold that was passed down through the family looks a lot like the gold from other mines in the area—same proportion of tin or silver or lead or copper or whatever. And then there's our family history backing up the assay. Case had a brother who married a girl he'd found running wild in mustang country. She was Mad Jack's friend. The country she ran in was just south of here. Since Mad Jack went everywhere on foot, it stands to reason that his mine is somewhere nearby. At least, that's what Cash figured seven years ago. He's been hunting that mine ever since, every chance he gets."

Luke leaned forward and took the coffee mug from Carla's fingers. He told himself that he hadn't meant to brush his hand over hers as he freed the mug, but he didn't believe it. He also told himself that he couldn't taste her on the mug's thick rim, and he didn't believe that, either. He took a sip, looked at her and smiled a slow, lazy kind of smile.

"You've been snitching chocolate chips from the cookie batter, haven't you?"

Carla made a startled sound, then flushed, realizing that somehow she had left a taste of chocolate on the mug.

"I'm sorry. I'll get my own cup."

"No," Luke said softly, holding Carla's chair in

place with his boot, making it impossible for her to push away from the table and stand. "I like the taste of…chocolate."

He watched the sudden intake of her breath and the leap of the pulse in her neck. When he looked at her mouth, the pink lips were slightly parted, surprise or invitation or both. Her eyes were wide and her pupils had dilated with sudden sensual awareness.

Luke drank, watching her over the rim, putting his mouth where hers had been and savoring the coffee all the more because of it. When he put the mug back in her fingers, he turned it so that when she lifted the mug to drink, her mouth would touch the same part of the rim his had.

"Drink," Luke said softly, "and I'll pour some more."

Unable to look away from him, Carla brought the mug to her mouth. When the warm rim brushed her lips it was as though Luke had kissed her. Carla's fingers trembled suddenly, forcing her to hold the mug with both hands as she sipped. The betraying tremor didn't escape the tawny eyes that were watching her so intently. When she lowered the mug and licked her lips, she heard the soft, tearing sound of Luke's quickly drawn breath. He took the mug from her again, poured coffee, sipped and then returned the mug to her.

"Case MacKenzie liked more than the land around here. He found a girl whose daddy hadn't been fast enough with a gun or lucky enough with a miner's pick. Mariah Turner had inherited water rights to Echo Canyon Creek, Wild Horse Springs and Ten Sentinels Seep, and mineral rights to a lot more country. She also had every outlaw in the whole damned territory camped on her doorstep.''

Carla closed her eyes and relaxed slowly as she listened to Luke's deep voice talk about people who had lived more than a century ago, people to whom the Four Corners country was a landscape both intimately encountered and nearly unknown, a wild place where white history was nonexistent and Indian history was so old that most of it had been long forgotten.

''I've seen pictures of Mariah,'' Luke said. ''I know why the outlaws were circling around howling at the moon. She was all woman. But she had more than a good body and a pretty face. She had the kind of guts that make a man want to catch moonlight and bring it to her in his cupped hands like water, just to see her smile.''

Luke sipped coffee while Carla watched, her breath held, tasting in her mind the coffee that was sliding over his tongue, wishing she could be that close to him just once before she died. Watching her, sensing what she was thinking, Luke handed the mug back to her and continued speaking.

''Mariah held on to the land and played outlaws off against one another like a nineteenth-century Queen Elizabeth, letting no man get the upper hand in her life. For two years the outlaws fought for her favors—and made sure that no man got close to her without being killed—and then her worst fears came true. An outlaw who was better with a gun than any of the others rode into her valley. The other outlaws couldn't take the man head-on and he was too quick and too wary to take by ambush.''

''What happened?''

''Mariah was lucky. The man was Case MacKenzie.''

''The one with the saddlebags full of gold?''

''The same.'' Luke smiled. ''He didn't plan to get married. He didn't even plan to fall in love. Yet before long he was writing notes to himself, talking about hair that was the color of dark mountain honey and sunlight all mixed together.'' Tawny, intent eyes moved over Carla's hair. ''Like your hair. Your eyes are like Mariah's too, clear and direct. And your mouth is like hers. The kind of mouth that makes a man want...''

Luke let his voice die away. He took the mug and sipped again, forcing himself not to say any more. The hint of chocolate left by Carla was sweeter than any kiss he had ever tasted.

''Maybe you've got Turner blood in you, sunshine. The more I look at you, the more you remind me of Mariah.'' Luke sighed and rubbed his neck with his right hand, cursing the luck that had him living with a woman he wanted and must not take. ''Mariah was the woman Case had been looking for in more ways than one. He had been trying to find Mad Jack Turner's son, to give him his share of his father's gold. Well, it was too late for Johnny Turner, but not for his daughter, Mariah. The gold was just what she needed to improve the Rocking M's beef stock, hire honest hands and make the place a real ranch instead of an outlaw roost.''

Luke laughed softly, remembering his father and grandfather telling the same story to him years ago. "And while Mariah was at it, she improved the human stock, too. She had eight children by the man no one could kill, the husband she called her 'beloved outlaw.' One of the kids was Matthew Case MacKenzie, my grandfather's father. Then came Lucas Tyrell MacKenzie, then my father, Samuel Matthew MacKenzie, and then me, Lucas Case MacKenzie. And the Rocking M came with the MacKenzie name, passed on to whichever son had the sand to make a go of ranching in this country.''

Carla looked at Luke's face, burned by wind and sun, dark from days without shaving, marked by fine lines radiating out from the corners of his eyes, lines left by a lifetime of looking into long distances and sunlight undimmed by city smoke. In his faded blue chambray shirt, worn jeans and scarred cowboy boots, Luke could have easily stepped out of the pages of his own family history.

"I'll bet you look like him," Carla said softly.

"My father?"

"No. The beloved outlaw. Case."

Something in Carla's voice made desire leap fiercely within Luke, but it was unlike any desire he had ever known. It was not only her sweet body and soft mouth he wanted; he also felt an almost over-powering need to hold her and be held by her in return, to hear her whisper that he was her beloved outlaw, the one man whom she had been born to love.

The one man she must not love, for he could not give her the life she deserved.

"I envy Mariah," Carla continued slowly. "She gave her outlaw everything a woman wants to give her man, and in doing so she became a part of the land every bit as much as the ancient ruins or the Indians who drew on Picture Cliff and then disappeared. Everyone always talks of the West as though it only belonged to cowboys and Indians and outlaws. It belonged to the women, too. In their own way, they fought just as fiercely for the land as any man ever did. I would like to have been a part of that."

"Don't kid yourself, schoolgirl," Luke said sardonically. "No matter how they start out, women end up hating this land, and with good reason. The country grinds them up like they were corn rubbed between two rocks."

"It didn't grind up Mariah Turner MacKenzie."

Luke shrugged and drank coffee. "She was one in a million. I've never envied any man anything, but I envy Case MacKenzie Mariah's love. He found a woman with enough sheer grit to take on this brutal, beautiful land and never cry for mama or silk sheets or the company of other women. Hell, I take it back—Mariah was one in *ten* million.''

"A lot of women lived in the West," Carla said evenly. "More than a fifth of the homestead claims were taken out by women who were alone."

Luke's eyebrows came up. "I didn't know that."

"Of course not. Men write history."

He smiled slightly, a flash of white against the dark beard stubble. Then the smile faded and he pinned Carla with his eyes. There was no desire in his glance now, no fire, nothing but the cold sheen of hammered metal.

"Case's son wasn't lucky. Matthew MacKenzie married a Denver girl. She was the youngest of a big family and she spent the first ten years of the marriage having babies and crying herself sick for mama. Two of her kids survived. By the time they were in their teens, she was back in Denver."

Luke took a sip of coffee and rotated the mug absently on the tabletop. Carla watched, afraid to speak, sensing that he was trying to tell her something but he didn't quite know how to go about it.

"Divorce was out of the question in those days. The two of them simply lived separately—he was on the ranch, she in the city. The boy, Lucas Tyrell MacKenzie, grew up and inherited the Rocking M," Luke continued. "He was my grandfather. He married the daughter of a local rancher. She had three kids and was pregnant with a fourth when her horse threw her. By the time he got her to a doctor, she and the baby were both dead. Eight years later my grandfather married again. Grandmother Alice hated the Rocking M. As soon as my father was old enough to run the place, my grandparents moved to Boulder.''

Carla listened without moving, hearing echoes of old anger and fresh despair in Luke's voice; and worst of all, the silent, unflinching monotone of a man who knew he could not have what he most wanted in life.

''Dad and his two brothers lived on the ranch. One after another they went to Korea. One after another they came home, married to women they had met, where they took their military training.''

Luke lifted the coffee mug again, realized it was empty and set it aside. He didn't need it. The rest of the MacKenzie story wouldn't take long to tell.

''It was a disaster,'' he said calmly. ''It had been hard enough to find a woman who would tolerate life on an isolated cattle ranch even in horse-and-buggy days. In the days of suburbia and flower children and moon shots, it was impossible. One of my uncles moved off the ranch and into town; his wife quit drinking and he started up. My other uncle refused to move to town. His wife made his life living hell. My two cousins and I used to sleep in the barn to get away from the arguments. One night my aunt couldn't take it anymore. My uncle had hidden the car keys, so she set out on foot for town. It was February. She didn't make it."

Luke's lips twisted down in a hard curve. "In any case, she got her wish. She never saw the sun set behind theFire Mountains again."

A chill moved over Carla's skin. She had heard enough bits and pieces about Luke's past to guess what was coming next. "Luke, you don't have to tell—"

"No," he interrupted, watching Carla with bleak yellow eyes. "I'm almost done. My mother hated the Rocking M from the moment she set foot on it. But she loved my father. She tried to make a go of it. She simply wasn't tough enough. At first we didn't even have a phone for her to talk to her family or friends. No women lived nearby. Nothing but kids and the kind of work that has broken stronger women than my mother ever was, even on her best day.

"One night the wind started screaming around the peaks and she started screaming right along with it. A week later her parents came for her. They took her, my sister and my cousins—both girls—and they went back east, saying the Rocking M wasn't a fit place for females. I never saw my sister again. She was seven. All I have of her is some old pictures and the doll I was mending for her. When they took her away I was out chasing strays. I didn't even get the chance to say goodbye. Afterward Dad set out to drink himself to death. He was a big man. It took him years, but he finally made it.''

"What about your mother?'' Carla asked unhappily.

"I hear she remarried. I never saw her again.''

Carla looked into Luke's bleak amber eyes and felt her own heart turn over with a need to hold him, comfort him, give him some warmth to offset his cold memories.

"Luke,'' she whispered.

Without thinking Carla pushed back from the table and went to Luke, taking his face in her hands, feeling the beard-roughened warmth of his cheeks against her palms. He sat motionless, but his eyes blazed within his silence. He made no effort either to pursue or to withdraw from her touch.

"Luke, I...''

Carla's voice died because she didn't know what to say.

"Luke,'' Carla breathed, bending down to his mouth, almost touching it with her own, trembling.

She had little experience to guide her, only her own need to know the heat and textures and taste of this one man. She could feel the rush of his breath over her lips, smell the coffee he had recently drunk, sense the warmth that waited for her finally within her reach. With aching slowness she lowered her head until her mouth brushed over his. She repeated the caress again, another brushing motion, and then again and again, and each time she lingered longer, pressed against his mouth a bit more, until finally she could feel the hardness of his teeth behind the warm resilience of his lips.

It was good, so very good, but it wasn't enough. Carla remembered how it had been to taste Luke. Hot, wildly exciting, transforming her in the few seconds before the kiss had become too adult, too hard, demanding more of her than she had dreamed at eighteen; but she had dreamed many, many times since then, and running through her dreams like streamers of fire had been the memory of his taste, the electric intimacy of his tongue caressing her own, the hard length of his body imprinted on her own softness.

Remembering how it had been three years ago, Carla slowly opened her mouth until she could touch Luke's lips with just the tip of her tongue. She felt the shock wave of sensation that went through him at the caress, making his powerful body tremble. A small whimper escaped from the back of her throat when she tried to breathe and found she couldn't; she was held in the vise of the sensual instant, wholly focused on the sensations spreading from the tip of her tongue throughout her body.

The sound of surprise and discovery that Carla made sent another shock wave moving through Luke, shaking him.

"Sunshine," he whispered, "oh, baby, don't..."

He had no breath to finish, for she had taken it from him with another gliding caress of her tongue.

The sound he made then was not unlike hers when she discovered she couldn't breathe. She trembled and moved her mouth again, instinctively fitting it more closely to his, touching his lips with her tongue, finding warmth, seeking the greater warmth she knew lay within.

Luke tried not to lift his arms, tried not to close them around Carla, tried not to turn and ease his legs between hers, tried not to pull her down until the soft weight of her was astride his thighs. But it happened anyway, the catching and the holding, the turning and the pulling down. It all happened in sweet, slow motion despite his desperate reluctance to allow any part of it to happen at all. His body simply ignored the commands of his mind, for the shy gliding of her tongue had taken away his ability to remember yesterday and foresee tomorrow.

There was enough self-control in Luke not to frighten Carla as he had three years ago, but not enough to turn her away as he knew he must. Like a mountain lying in wait for dawn, poised in the instants between darkness and light, Luke let Carla come to him—first the faint hint of warmth, then the delicate pressure of sunshine sliding down his body to rest in his lap, sending heat radiating through him. He whispered her name again, a word more felt than heard, for it was breathed from his mouth into hers.

The piercing sweetness of hearing him say her name was greater than anything Carla had dreamed, making her shiver and cry out, a cry that went no farther than the dark warmth of Luke's mouth. Moments later he felt the gentle scalding of her tears against his lips and was racked by emotion himself. To be wanted like that was more than he had believed possible, even in his hottest dreams.

Trembling, pressing closer and closer to the heat and power of Luke's body, Carla touched his tongue with her own, wanting the taste of him to fill her mouth as it had once before. She felt the sudden, fierce clenching of his thighs as she settled more fully onto his lap, pressing lightly against him with her breasts and hips and belly. And still the kiss stayed gentle, almost fragile, balanced on the blazing edge of fire.

She wanted to tell him that it was all right, that this time she wouldn't turn and run if he kissed her back, kissed her hard, kissed her as though he were dying of thirst and she was a clear spring for his taking. But she said nothing, for in order to speak she would have had to end the kiss...and that she could not do. She had dreamed of this too long, too completely, dreaming all the way down to her soul.

So Carla kissed Luke as she wanted to be kissed, tasting him deeply, feeling the sweet abrasion of beard stubble at the edges of his lips and beneath her palms, pressing closely, sinking into him, trembling, feeling him tremble in return. His mouth opened as he both allowed her greater freedom and took her own mouth in return. His tongue slid between her teeth, tasted her in wild silence, found every hidden softness of her mouth and then slowly, slowly began an intimate rhythm of penetration and retreat.

The languid stroking was repeated by his big hands smoothing up and down her back, her legs, easing her closer, shifting her hips with gentle pressures, lifting her body into more perfect balance with his; and all the while he continued the complete seduction of her mouth, making it wholly his. Her tongue moved in rhythm with his, she tasted of him, her breath tore as his did, and the small sounds of passion he drew from the back of her throat were the essence of his own desire.

Luke's hands clenched and his short nails raked with sensuous precision down Carla's spine. He felt the breaking of her breath, the wild shudder of her body, the involuntary arching of her hips into his. He tried to bite back a cry of pleasure-pain as she rocked softly against his aroused flesh, but a groan escaped his control; and she drank the passionate sound as he had drunk her own small cries.

The warmth of Luke's hands followed the slow unbuttoning of Carla's blouse, and as each button came undone his teeth sank gently into her tongue, distracting her. She would have let him undress her anyway, distraction or no, for her skin was on fire and her clothes were stifling her and she wanted to be as naked as her tongue sweetly tangling with his.

Luke had just enough self-control left to know if he unhooked Carla's bra, he wouldn't stop undressing her until she was wholly nude, her body open to him, and he was naked within her. With hands that shook, he pushed aside the soft folds of cotton blouse and smoothed his palms over her breasts once, lightly.

He might as well have taken a whip of fire to her. She shivered, transfixed, and her nipples hardened to his soft touch.

Knowing he shouldn't, helpless to prevent himself, Luke slid a long finger beneath each bra strap and slowly caressed her the hollow of Carla's collarbone to the warm slope of her breasts. He hesitated, groaned almost soundlessly and eased his fingers farther down, beneath the warm lace, stroking slowly, savoring the rise of warm, firm flesh, the satin areola, the velvet of her nipples. Sweetly, in the same rhythm as his tongue mating with hers, he flicked back and forth over the tight peaks beneath the lace until they were as hard as the male flesh thrusting hungrily between his thighs.

A soft, ragged moan was torn from Carla's lips, a sound Luke took into his own mouth, devouring it as he wanted to devour her. For long, rasping seconds he plucked her velvet nipples until she quivered wildly and her hips rocked in silent pleading against his hard flesh. He freed one hand and let it slide over her belly, tracing the zipper of her jeans without opening it, sliding down and down until he could feel her humid heat resting in the palm of his hand. He moved slowly, rocking with her, wanting her until it was like dying not to take her.

With a sound of anguish Luke ended the kiss, freeing his mouth without freeing Carla's body from his caressing hands. She trembled violently, breathing as raggedly as he was, her eyes dark with the first passion she had ever known.

"I want you," Luke said harshly, flexing his hand into Carla's secret warmth, shuddering when she moaned. "But that's all it will ever be," he continued through clenched teeth, understanding finally the dimensions of his own personal hell. "Wanting. No rings and vows, no babies and color snapshots and scrapbooks to put in with the old albums. No happily ever after. I'll grind no modern woman into bits on the Rocking M. I'll leave no more children to be raised without mothers. The MacKenzie line will end with me."

Shocked, trembling, trying not to cry, Carla felt Luke's pain more deeply than her own.

"But I want you to know this," he continued, his voice savage, his eyes blazing with all he would never know, never do, never be. "No matter who you marry or how many lovers you take, no matter how long you live, no man will ever want you the way I do."

With a swift, powerful movement Luke stood, lifting Carla and setting her aside in the same motion.

"Stay away from me, sunshine. If you come to

me again like this I'm afraid I won't have the strength to say no. Then I would take you and hate you and myself and the ranch that's as much a part of me as my soul.''

9

"Cosy just left," Luke said, answering Carla's question and watching her intently despite the activity around the corral. "Why? Did you want to go to town with him?"

Carla shook her head, making a shaft of sunlight tangle and run through her hair. "I've got a recipe I want to try and it needs a particular spice. By the time I realized it, it was too late to put in on the list."

Luke snapped his leather work gloves impatiently against his thigh. "Hell, schoolgirl, this is a ranch, not a fancy city restaurant. West Fork never heard of most of the junk you want to put in the food."

Carla's chin came up as belligerently as Luke's. "Listen, cowboy, the only complaint I've ever had from the men about my cooking is that their horses are threatening to go on strike over all the extra poundage they have to haul around these days."

A corner of Luke's mouth turned up. "Heard rumors of that myself. Even Ten ordered a new pair of jeans, and that old boy was nothing but rawhide and hard times before he started putting away your food like there was no tomorrow. First thing you know he'll be as fat as I am.''

''You? Fat?'' Carla looked Luke over from the brim of his cowboy hat to the toes of his boots. ''Pull my other leg. There's not an extra ounce on you anywhere. You and Ten are enough to make me yank my hair out. The more I feed you, the better you look, and Lord knows neither one of you was exactly ugly to begin with.''

Luke laughed despite the stabbing pleasure Carla's frank admiration sent through him. He had tried to keep her at arm's length since she had come to him in the blazing silence of the dining room and taught him just how much a man could want a woman and still survive not having her. He had twenty-three more days of hell to endure until her stint as cook and housekeeper was over.

Twenty-three days. He wondered if he could make it. Keeping Carla at a distance had proven to be impossible. The anger he had turned against her earlier in the summer was simply gone, burned up in the far hotter fires of his passion for her. He was edgy, he slept badly, he was short-tempered—but not with Carla. No matter how much easier it would have been to be angry with her, he simply could not feel rage toward the girl who had come to him, offering her body and her soul to him with a single shattering kiss.

One kiss, but no more. Carla had heeded Luke's pain, if not his warning. She continued to serve Luke hot food when he came in long after the other hands had eaten. She poured coffee for him, joined him if he asked her to, listened with transparent pleasure when he talked about what he had done that day. She cleaned every inch of the house, washed and mended everything in his closet and drawers. She joked with all the men equally, giving no man any encouragement to become personal, and did it all so diplomatically that Luke was reminded of Mariah Turner's deft handling of the courting outlaws.

In all, Carla had done nothing to earn Luke's displeasure and everything to fulfill the terms of the bet. He could hardly blame her if sometimes he turned around unexpectedly and saw her watching him with desire and wonder mingling in her beautiful eyes. He watched her in the same way, was caught in the same way, and walked off in the same way.

Alone.

Nothing was said. No excuse was given. None was needed. Luke and Carla could not have understood each other better if they had been connected to the same central nervous system.

And time after time, late at night, when thunder and lightning stalked the wild land, Luke heard Carla pacing her room, then tiptoeing down the hall to the kitchen. A few minutes later he would hear the faint scrape of a dining room chair being moved; and he would lie awake, his body clenched with savage need, and picture how she must look at that instant, sitting and sipping hot lemon water, wearing nothing but the black shirt he had left with Cash...the shirt Carla had chosen to use as a nightgown, wearing nothing beneath it but her fragrant skin.

Sometimes it was Luke who awakened, paced and went to the kitchen for something warm and soothing. Sometimes it was Luke who scraped a dining room chair over linoleum and sat shirtless, his jeans half-buttoned, with nothing under the jeans but his rigid, intractable hunger for his best friend's kid sister.

"I'd better do the breakfast dishes," Carla said.

She turned away, unable to bear the intensity of Luke's eyes a moment longer. Yet even with her back turned, she felt him watching her as she went to the house. The thought of leaving tomorrow with Cash for September Canyon was all that kept her from throwing back her head and screaming in a combination of frustration and...frustration. She had thought there could be no worse punishment than loving a man who didn't love her.

She had been wrong. Wanting a man who wanted but refused to take her was worse. Much worse. She felt his unhappiness as acutely as her own.

Do you feel my pain, Luke? Is that why your eyes

follow me, watching every step, every breath, every gesture?

Don't do that. Don't watch me. Don't look at my mouth and remember how it felt to kiss me so deeply that we tasted of each other long after the kiss ended. Stop torturing yourself. Stop torturing me.

Twenty-three more days. God, how can I do it? And how can I not?

Forcing herself not to think about it, Carla went to the kitchen and frowned over the recipe she wanted to make that night for the men. It was a French recipe for beef stew that had a long, elegant name. But she lacked one of the pungent herbs she needed. She reread the ingredient list again, went to the cupboard and sighed. The closest she could come was sage, which was already in the recipe.

"If only it were pine nuts," she muttered, flipping pages, looking for another recipe, "there would be no problem. I'd just go up the trail to MacKenzie Ridge and shake down some ripe piñon cones and spent the next three days getting the sap out of my hair."

Remembering, Carla laughed. But it had been worth it to see the look on the men's faces when they asked what the tasty crunchy things in the green beans were. She only wished Luke had been there to share the joke, but it had been during the time he had spent days camping out, scouring the ranch for something he never named.

Suddenly Carla remembered the juniper branch

that Luke had brought to her yesterday, saying he thought she might like the smell of it in her room. The deep green of the needles had been studded with the small, powdery silver blue of the hard berries. Flipping quickly to the index of the cookbook, Carla looked up juniper, found a recipe in which it was used and discovered that a very few berries went a long way in flavoring any stew. She closed the book, ran upstairs to her room and returned with several pungent berries in her hand. Singing softly to herself, she began assembling the ingredients for *boeuf à la campagne*.

By dinnertime the smells emanating from the ranch house were enough to make a hungry man weak. As usual when Luke wasn't around at dinnertime, Ten was the first man in the door by a good forty minutes. He looked at the stove, noted that she was using the big pot again and crossed the kitchen quickly.

"I'll take care of that," he said.

"Thanks, but I can—"

"Want to get me fired?" Ten interrupted, taking the heavy pot from Carla's hands, pot holders and all.

"Of course not!"

"Then make real sure I do the heavy lifting when Luke isn't around or he'll have my butt for a saddle blanket. He was very particular about not having you wrestle with gallons of boiling stuff."

The realization that Luke had told Ten to help her made emotions shiver invisibly through Carla.

"Thank you," she said huskily. "I have to admit I've been thinking of rigging a block and tackle for the stove."

Ten smiled as he set the pot full of stew on the worn counter. "Smells like heaven."

She gave him a sideways look. "I'd have guessed you were more familiar with *un*heavenly smells."

He laughed and began filling two huge serving dishes with stew, using a ladle the size of a soup plate. Smiling, Carla turned back to her other dinner preparations, grateful for Ten's quiet help...and at the same time unable to keep from wishing that it were Luke's hands lifting the heavy pots, Luke's arms flexing with casual strength, Luke's broad shoulders making the kitchen seem small.

"Is Luke coming in for dinner?" Carla asked two seconds after telling herself she wouldn't.

"Nope."

"Is he...camping again?"

"Not this time. Some fool cow took a notion to tangle with barbed wire. Luke will walk her to the barn after he sews her up a bit." Ten looked up at the clock. "Be a few hours yet."

"Ladle some of that into the small pot, would you?" Carla asked. "I'll keep it warm for him."

"You're spoiling him shamefully."

She shrugged. "Just doing my job."

"None of the other cooks ever kept food warm for the man who worked through dinner."

"From what I've heard, none of them cooked anything worth keeping warm," Carla said dryly.

Ten bent over the ladle and inhaled. "Damn, but that smells really fine. What's in it?"

"You wouldn't believe me."

"Sure I would."

"The usual things, plus bourbon and juniper berries."

Ten blinked. He sniffed again. "Juniper berries?"

"Think of them as Rocking M peppercorns."

"You think of them. I'm going to eat before you tell me something I don't want to know."

Cosy's voice called plaintively from the next room. "Hey, ramrod, you planning on sharing any of that with the men what do the real work or are you going to keep it all for yourself?"

"Don't get your water hot," Ten retorted. "If we fed you on the basis of work, you'd have starved to death long before now."

Carla just managed to remove the smile from her face before she walked into the dining room carrying a tray of steaming biscuits and a pot of dark mountain honey. Ten followed with the big bowls of stew. The food vanished shortly after it was put on the table.

The speed with which Carla's cooking disappeared no longer appalled her, for she had become accustomed to thinking in terms of feeding men who routinely burned three and four thousand calories a day. During roundup, branding, calving and other seasonally demanding kinds of work, the men would work sixteen-hour days, during which they would eat a minimum of four big meals and all the "snacks" they could cram into their pockets, saddlebags or the glove compartments of their pickup trucks.

Before Carla sat down to eat, she went back to the kitchen with the stew bowls, filling them again from the much-reduced volume of the cooking pot. After bringing the new bowls of stew, plus coffee refills, two more trays of biscuits and a new pot of honey, she sat down and ate her own dinner.

She didn't lack for company; the men who weren't polishing off second helpings were working their way through a third plate. By the time she had eaten her first—and only—serving, the men were through eating. It was the part of the meal Carla enjoyed most, for the full, satisfied men tended to sharpen their wits on one another while she brought in dessert.

Sometimes it was Carla who came in for her share of ribbing, but she enjoyed even that. It reminded her of the good-natured give-and-take she and Cash shared—and Luke, too, until that disastrous summer.

"What's this I hear about you running off tomorrow and leaving us to starve?" Cosy asked as he mopped up the last of the savory gravy with a biscuit.

"True," Carla said cheerfully. "I've saved up some days off."

"And you're going to run off to the city and never think of the brokenhearted boys you left behind."

"Actually," Carla said, standing up and gathering dirty plates, "I'm running off to September Canyon."

"Same difference," mumbled Cosy.

"It is?"

"Sure. We'll starve just the same."

"You can live off the fat of the land," Ten pointed out to Cosy.

"Speak for yourself, boy. I'm trim as a rattle-snake and twice as mean."

"Three times as ugly, too," called Jones from the end of the table. As the other men laughed, Jones kicked back and lit up a cigarette, sending a streamer of smoke across the table. "But that's still one hard-hearted woman," he added, gesturing toward Carla with a burned match. "Leaving us to starve and not turning a hair over it."

"Hate to disappoint you boys," Carla said, pausing in the doorway with her arms loaded with dishes, "but I doubled up on everything I made this week and froze half. You won't starve."

Shaking his head, Jones rocked back from the table and blew out another stream of smoke. When Carla returned and began passing out dessert, Jones watched her closely and said as though no time had passed, "It's not the same a'tall. Nothing's as good as fresh." He gave Carla a thorough, up-and-down look and took another drag on his cigarette. "'Course, I might forgive you if you gave me a big kiss before you leave."

"Nope," Carla said instantly, hearing Ten's chair creak as he turned toward the brash young hand.

"You sure about that?" Jones asked, blowing out smoke again, looking at her with open appraisal. "Bet I could change your mind, little darling."

"Not a chance. Nothing personal, but kissing you would be like licking an ashtray."

The men laughed loudly. After a moment, Jones shook his head and laughed, too. Ten's smile flickered very briefly, but there was a look in his eyes that told Carla a ranch hand called Jones would be hearing the rough edge of his ramrod's tongue. And, she admitted to herself, it might be just as well; during the past few weeks she had become increasingly aware of Jones. Of all the hands, he was the only one she took care not to be alone with. It was nothing he had said or done; she simply didn't like the way he looked at her.

Ten lingered while, one by one, the other men finished dessert. The hands had taken to carrying their dirty dishes into the kitchen after a meal, which saved Carla a lot of running back and forth. There was usually some more good-humored joking as the hands grabbed a final cup of coffee before going to the bunkhouse for a night of cards, TV, VCR movies or a few rounds on the battered old pool table.

Ten rolled up his sleeves and began scraping dishes. While he did it, he kept an eye on the men who came and went from the kitchen. Especially Jones. The hands sensed their ramrod's displeasure. No one lingered tonight. They carried in dishes, grabbed a cup of coffee, and vanished.

Carla waited until everyone had left before she turned to Ten and said neutrally, "The way you're snarling, not one of those hands is going to so much as say good-night to me from now on."

Ten smiled slowly. "The men understand. They can go so far and no farther."

"Fine," Carla said, irritated by the feeling of being protected beyond any reasonable need. "But what would happen if I wanted to get to know one of the men better?"

For an instant there was silence. Then, "Do you?"

She threw up her hands. "That's not the point."

"Sure it is."

"But—"

"Think of it this way," Ten said, interrupting calmly. "If you did want to get to know one of the hands better, you'd be doing him a real favor if you left the Rocking M and took him with you. Otherwise, he'd be a mighty sorry puppy about the time Luke turned up and started hammering out postholes with him. You don't want some nice, stupid boy on your conscience, do you?"

"Is it so awful just to want to have fun with somebody?"

"Try Luke."

"I'd love to," Carla shot back. Hearing the stark emotion in her own voice made her wince. "Never mind, Ten. Guess I'm just—" she shrugged "—ragged. I'm looking forward to my time off."

"Yeah, I'll bet cooking for this bunch of wolves can get real wearing."

She shook her head. "Cooking, no. Cleaning? Amen."

The outside door to the kitchen slammed behind Luke. "Then stick with cooking, schoolgirl. We're not having a fancy dress ball or white glove inspection here anytime soon," he said, tossing his hat onto the counter. "If you wax the closet floor once more I'll break my neck reaching for shirts." He threw Ten a cool look. "Working late?"

"Just following orders."

Luke went wholly still. "Who's crowding her?"

"Jones," Ten said.

"No," Carla said quickly. "It's not like that. He hasn't done anything."

Luke looked at Ten.

The ramrod shook his head, disagreeing with Carla.

Luke nodded abruptly and said to Ten, "I'll draw his pay. Have him off the Rocking M by noon tomorrow."

"Luke," Carla said urgently, "you can't fire a

ranch hand just because he made a joke about kissing me.''

"Like hell I can't.'' He glared down at Carla with narrow golden eyes. "Jones has a bad reputation with women.''

"So does Ten, according to you,'' Carla pointed out tightly.

"Not like Jones. Ten never took anything that wasn't offered. Jones did, and maybe more than once. He got off easy because the gal wasn't exactly a virgin to begin with, but that doesn't change what happened. Even a prostitute has the right to say no to a man.''

Carla started to speak but was too shocked.

"I hired Jones because there aren't any women on the Rocking M and he's a top hand when he isn't drinking and trying to prove he's God's gift to girls. Then you came here. Jones swore to me he wouldn't drink and he wouldn't so much as look at you. I haven't caught him looking, but I'm not so sure about the booze.''

Luke glanced at Ten, who nodded.

"Thought I smelled it on him yesterday in the pasture,'' Luke muttered, rubbing his neck angrily. "Damn it to *hell*. Tell Cosy to drive Jones into West Fork tonight. Tell Jones not to come back. Ever.''

"He'll want to hear it from you,'' Ten said.

"You really think he's that stupid?'' Luke asked hopefully, watching Ten with the eyes of a cougar.

The ramrod's smile was slow and savage. "Probably not. Too bad. You've been spoiling for a fight. Couldn't happen to a nicer guy than Jones.''

"Yeah. I should have fired that SOB the second I knew Carla was coming here. Females and the Rocking M. Nothing but trouble.''

"And good cooking," Ten added. "Don't forget that. Carla's got more of those chocolate chip cookies you favor stashed in the freezer. Nothing like a good woman to spoil a man, is there?''

"While it lasts, no. But when she's gone—and she always goes—it just makes the hard times harder.''

10

The kitchen door snapped shut behind Ten, leaving Carla and Luke alone in the taut silence. Silently she watched while Luke went to the sink, rolled up his sleeves and began washing up. He rinsed dust off his face, soaped all the way up his muscular forearms to his elbows and used a nailbrush on his hands. That was one of the things Carla had always noticed about Luke; no matter how hard he had worked or how tired he was, he always came to her table with clean hands.

And such handsome hands they were, almost elegant despite their large size. Long, lean fingers and neatly trimmed nails. A hand deft enough to pick a tiny flower without bruising it and strong enough to lift a saddle one-handed and lower it onto a cow pony's back. Luke's hands fascinated her. Warm, hard, capable of trembling with desire and yet still touching her with restraint, sensitive enough to measure and savor all the textures of her breasts, caressing her nipples from softness to velvet pebbles.

"Did I miss some dirt?"

Carla's head snapped up to meet Luke's eyes. "What?"

"You were staring at my hands."

"I..." Carla's voice died. She closed her eyes, unable to bear the exquisite torture of looking at Luke's hands any longer and remembering how it had felt to be touched by him, if only for a few moments. "I'll see if your dinner is still warm."

"You mean the wolves left some scraps for me?"

"I stood over the stew with a shotgun."

He smiled. "Did you eat?"

"A little."

He hesitated, then said slowly, as though against his better judgment, "Keep me company and I'll help you finish off the dishes."

"Sold," Carla said instantly. Her blue-green eyes appreciated Luke's smile and noted the signs of a long day's work in his face. "But you don't have to do my job, too. You look like you've been working so hard that you're too tired to sleep properly."

Luke's eyes narrowed. He wondered if Carla had heard him prowling the kitchen for the past three nights. When he was awake he could banish the memory of her body pressed to his, but when he slept, it was different. In his dreams he sat half-clothed in the dining room and she came to him, laughter and sunshine and sensual heat that bathed

him in passion until he cried out; and then he awakened alone, sweating, his breath a tearing sound in
the darkness.

"Sit down," Carla said. "I'll bring dinner to you.
You must be starved."

Luke barely kept himself from saying he would
rather have Carla than any dinner on earth; and he
would rather have her in the dining room, sitting
astride his lap, her head thrown back, her nipples
taut and glistening from his mouth, her body sheath-
ing him, bringing him relief from the torment of
wanting her.

"Whatever you give me always tastes good,"
Luke said finally, trying not to watch Carla's mouth
too hungrily.

The look in his golden eyes made her breath
catch. A delicate, invisible shiver went from her
breastbone to the pit of her stomach.

At that instant Carla realized that she should put
Luke's dinner on the table, return immediately to
the kitchen and finish the dishes, leaving him to eat
alone. Then she should go put one of the Rocking
M's movie cassettes on the VCR and watch it.
Alone. Or she should read one of her own or Luke's
many books on archaeology and the history of the
West, or she should make more casseroles and cookies for the men to eat while she was camping in
September Canyon, or…anything but sit in aching
silence watching Luke eat, envying the very food
that touched his lips.

"Go sit down," Carla said huskily. "I'll bring you dinner."

She brought Luke's food to him, sat down with him, watched him eat and envied the food that touched his lips. The silence was both electric and oddly companionable. Not until Luke had had time to appease the worst of his hunger did Carla begin asking him about his day.

"Did you see more cougar tracks around the Wildfire Canyon seep?"

He nodded and smiled to himself. "Looks like she has herself at least one cub, maybe two."

"You aren't going to hunt her," Carla said, reading Luke's expression and the nuances of his voice.

It was a statement rather than a question, but Luke answered Carla anyway, thinking aloud as he had become accustomed to doing with her in the quiet hours after the long day's work was done.

"The cat's in pretty close to the ranch buildings," Luke said slowly. Then he shrugged. "I'll probably regret it, but I won't touch her unless she starts living off calves instead of deer. There's a big part of me that likes knowing cougars have come back to the lower canyons to live the way they did when Case MacKenzie rode into the country."

"Like the wild black stallion?" Carla asked.

"Well," Luke drawled, rubbing his cheek, "you can't prove by me that that old stud is alive in anything but Ten's mind. Cougars, now...I've seen cougars."

Luke sipped coffee, then leaned back in his chair, relaxing and enjoying the peaceful moment. "I think cougars must be the prettiest cat God ever made. Quick, quiet, moving smooth as water, with eyes that remind men we aren't the only life worth caring about on earth. There were wild animals a long time before there were cities. And if we don't screw it up, there will be wild animals a long time after humans get smart and plow the cities under."

Carla smiled softly at Luke. "Do you suppose the Anasazi sat inside their stone apartment buildings and listened to cougars scream?"

"Wouldn't surprise me, especially in the higher canyons. But I'm sure the Anasazi heard coyotes wherever they built." Luke looked up from his coffee and caught Carla watching him with blue-green eyes full of longing. "Did you hear them last night, crying to the moon?"

"Yes. I stood by the window and listened for a long time."

"So did I."

Carla looked into Luke's tawny eyes and felt delicate splinters of sensation quiver through her. In her mind she saw Luke standing by his bedroom window, his body bare of all but moonlight, his eyes reflecting the limitless, elemental night; and all around him, surrounding him, was the mysterious song of coyotes. In her mind she was standing there with him, sharing his warmth, wearing only cool moonlight on her skin...moonlight and the memory of what it had been like to feel Luke's caress. Without knowing it, she shivered.

Luke's hand tightened around his fork until his knuckles showed white. It was a physical effort for him not to reach out and pull Carla onto his lap once more, kissing her once more, caressing her breasts once more; but this time he would remove her jeans and know her soft heat for the first time, nothing between his hunger and the wild, sweet melting of her body at his touch.

"So damned beautiful," he whispered. "And so damned impossible to have."

Carla blinked and focused on the present instead of on her timeless sensual dreams. "What?"

For an instant Luke didn't respond. When he spoke it was only half the truth, for the other half was too painful to speak aloud.

"The night," he said huskily. "It's beautiful. It could be yesterday or tomorrow or a thousand years ago. Some things never change. Like mountains and moonlight."

And man and woman. You and me.

The words rang so clearly in Carla's mind that she was afraid she had spoken them aloud. But Luke's expression didn't change. He continued to watch her with eyes like a cougar's—tawny, intent, deep with things that were impossible to name or speak aloud. Yet like the mountain lion stalking eternity in the rippling canyon shadows, Luke was connected to the intangible, indescribable, indestructible reality of the land itself.

"And like the canyons steeped in sunlight and sage," Luke continued slowly. "Like ancient trails snaking up steep rock walls, wild maize watered by thunderstorms, stone canyons older than human memory. Things that last, all of them. Things with staying power. The land demands it. That's why most people live in cities and look for cheap thrills. It's easier. No staying power required. But they'll never know what it's like to stand and look out over a canyon and feel yourself deeply rooted in the past, with the sunlight of ten thousand days locked in your body and your life branching into the future like the land itself."

Although Luke said nothing more, Carla knew he was thinking of his mother and his aunts and his grandmother, women whom the land had ground to dust and blown away on the relentless canyon winds. She wanted to touch him, to hold him, to tell him that the land lived in her soul as it did in his.

"Luke—"

"This is good stew," he said simultaneously, talking over Carla. "I suppose it has a fancy French name."

For a few seconds she fought against the change of subject. Then she looked at Luke's empty plate, freeing herself from the golden intensity of his eyes.

"Boeuf à la campagne," she admitted.

"Country beef, huh? Stew by any other name is still beef and gravy."

Carla blinked at Luke's accurate translation before she remembered that he had a fine arts degree from the University of Colorado. He also had a library of literature and history books that provided him with entertainment more often than the TV programs dragged from the sky by the Rocking M's satellite dish. Yet his western drawl and easy use of cowboy idioms had fooled more than one prospective beef buyer into believing that Luke had the intelligence and sophistication of a panfried steak.

"You and Ten are complete frauds, you know," she said. "Cowboys, my foot."

"Why, whatever do you mean, little bit?" Luke drawled, then spoiled it by laughing.

He settled more deeply against the back of the dining room chair, realizing as he did that evenings had become his favorite part of the day, especially when he worked late and had Carla all to himself. He enjoyed her quickness of mind and easy silences and her laughter when he told her fragments of the Rocking M's humorous lore—the dance hall girls and the Sisters of Sobriety watching one another from the corner of their eyes while a half-drunk pet pig sat outside the church, waiting for its completely drunk master to finish wrestling the devil and go home.

"Boeuf à la campagne," Luke repeated, shaking his head, smiling. "Hell of a thing to serve to a

cowboy." Then he paused, remembering what had happened that morning. "Isn't that what you wanted to make but didn't have the ingredients for?"

"I did a little creative substituting."

"Yeah? What did you use?"

"Juniper berries and bourbon."

Luke blinked. "Really?"

"Jest as shore as God made l'il green apples," she drawled broadly. "Rightly speaking, I cain't call it *boeuf à la campagne* no more. More like Rocking M stew. Better 'n possum, an' thet's God's own truth."

Luke's smile widened and then he laughed without restraint. So did Carla. For a few moments he felt as though he had been transported back to the time when he and Carla and Cash had sat around the old house's rickety table long after dinner, talking and teasing and just enjoying one another's company. It was as close to feeling part of a loving family as Luke had ever come.

Then he had ruined it by falling on Carla like a starving cougar on a rabbit. The fact that she had offered herself to him with her eyes full of girlish dreams only made his actions worse. He should have told her gently that he was honored, but it was impossible. He should have sent her on her way with her pride intact, if not her dreams. But he hadn't. He had kissed her too hard and then had shredded her with a few savage words when she panicked.

So she had avoided him for the past three years

and had come back to him this summer only to exorcise the girlish dreams of the past. And him. He didn't blame her for wanting to cut him out of her life, but he would spend the rest of his life wishing he had handled her differently. Then he could at least have continued to enjoy the undemanding companionship she brought to him, a sharing of thoughts and experiences that he had never come close to having with another woman.

Sex he could have from any number of females. Peace was something he had known only with Carla.

Sunshine.

Luke didn't know he had said the word aloud until he saw the sudden expansion of Carla's pupils as she watched him questioningly. He stood up with a controlled violence that hinted at the turbulence beneath his impassive exterior.

Who are you trying to kid, cowboy? Luke asked himself derisively. *You want more than conversation and good cooking from Carla. You want everything she has to give to a man, and you want it as hard and as hot and as deep as possible.*

Yes. And that's why I'll stay the hell away from her. I've gone this long without having her. I can go the rest of my life. What I couldn't survive would be watching the light in her eyes killed by the one thing in life that I love—this savage land.

She loves the ranch. She's said so more than once.

Sure. For a few weeks every summer. Big deal.

She's been here a lot longer than a few weeks.

Not once has she whined about not having anything to do or anyone to talk to or anything else. Hell, she's not even planning on going into town on her days off. She's going camping with Cash.

Wait until winter. Wait until the weather closes down and there's no way in hell to get off the Rocking M.

Luke's inner argument ended as though cut off by a knife. The horrifying harmony of his mother's screams rising and falling with the wind still echoed through his nightmares. He would never subject someone he cared about to that kind of torment.

Never.

11

There was no one about, no one near, no one in the world but Luke bending down to Carla, enveloping her in his warmth. His arms closed around her and she trembled even as she locked her arms around him. There was nothing under her feet, nothing over her head; she was spinning slowly, slowly, and he was spinning with her, holding her close, moving against her with sweet friction while around them a campfire burned in the slow rhythms of consummation, setting fire to the world, tongues of fire everywhere, everything burning and spinning and burning, she was burning—

Carla's eyes opened and her hands clenched the sheets as the aftermath of the dream twisted through her body. Her breath was broken, her skin hot, her body aching everywhere Luke had touched her weeks ago, touching her for only a few moments before setting her aside and telling her never to offer herself to him again.

*I'm afraid I won't have the strength to say no.
Then I would take you and hate you...*

Beyond the window, dawn spread down Mac-
Kenzie Ridge's black slopes, bathing the shadowed
land in the colors of life. Restlessly Carla threw back
the covers and got up. She was reaching for her
clothes when she remembered that today was the
beginning of her time off. Smoothing Luke's black
shirt around her hips, she went back to bed.

Sleep was impossible. She had slept little last
night, and if the sounds Luke made as he paced from
bedroom to living room to kitchen and back again
were any indication, he had slept no better than she
had.

Trying not to think, trembling as the aftermath of
her burning dream rippled through her, Carla lay and
listened to the sounds in the ranch house. The upper
story was quiet, which meant that Luke had already
showered and gone downstairs. The smell of coffee
permeated the house, which meant that someone—
probably Luke—had made coffee. The back door
into the kitchen snapped shut, and then she heard
male voices. The words were not distinguishable,
but she knew that Ten had arrived and was ribbing
Luke about something.

The door to the dining room had a distinctive
squeak. Carla heard it many times in the next hour
as she turned restlessly in bed, first to one side and
then the other, back to front to side to back, but
never comfortable for long. She told herself that the

smell of ham and eggs and hot cereal was making her too hungry to sleep, but she knew better. She was straining to hear Luke's voice, wondering if he were any less withdrawn this morning than he had been last night, when he had stood up abruptly and left the table.

Carla still couldn't believe her small joke about cowboys and drawls had offended Luke. He had laughed harder than she had. Then he had looked at her with an intensity that had made her weak. Before she could reach out to him, before she could do so much as blink, he stood up and walked out of the room.

Oh, Luke, don't you see how good we could be together? I can talk to you better than I can to anyone, even Cash. I can laugh and listen and you can do the same with me. We don't even have to be in the same room to enjoy being together. Just sitting and reading in the same house with you is better than going out with men I don't care about.

Don't turn away from me, Luke. Let me show you that I'm more like Mariah MacKenzie than I am like your mother.

The words ran over and over through Carla's mind in a litany of pain.

"Stop it, Carla McQueen," she finally told herself aloud. "Just stop it. You can't make someone love you, and if you aren't old enough to know it, you should be!"

The hissed ferocity of her own words joined the

unhappy thoughts that were turning in Carla's mind. She had come here to exorcise Luke so that she would be able to get on with her life, to date and fall in love like other girls.

But cutting Luke from her heart and mind had proven to be impossible. Each shared moment of laughter, each smile, each conversation, each gentle silence, each day she spent close to Luke embedded him more deeply in her soul. Last night it had taken a frightening amount of self-control not to run after him. She didn't know if she had the strength to hold back her emotions any longer, yet she couldn't bear a repetition of what had happened three years ago, when she had declared her love and had been told she wasn't old enough to know how to love a man.

Schoolgirl.

Slowly Carla realized that it had been many minutes since she had heard anyone moving around the house. The hands must have finished breakfast and gone about their work. She turned to the table next to her bed. The small travel clock told her that Cash was still several hours away from the Rocking M. Even worse, she had nothing to do to make the time pass faster. She had been packed and ready to go to September Canyon for three days. All she needed was her brother's arrival.

With a sound of impatience Carla pushed off the bed covers and got up. She paced the room aimlessly for a few minutes before she paused in front of the dresser. She ran her fingers caressingly over the wood's finely polished surface. After a moment, her hand went to the small carved ebony box that traveled with her everywhere. Smooth, graceful, elegant in its curving lines, the box had been a gift from Luke on her sixteenth birthday. Though he had said nothing, she suspected he had made it for her, just as he had made Cash a miniature display cabinet for gold nuggets.

Carla used the box to hold her most valued possession. Not jewelry, but a simple shard of pottery, another gift from Luke. She had been fourteen and recently orphaned when he had given the odd gift to her. She had never forgotten that moment or the tawny depths of his eyes or his deep, gentle voice trying to reach past her terrible loss and give her what comfort he could.

I found this in September Canyon and thought of you. You can look at this bit of clay and know that a long time ago a woman shaped a pot, decorated it, fed her family from it, maybe even passed it on to her children or her children's children. One day the pot broke and another pot was made and another family was fed until that pot broke and another was made in a cycle as old as life. It's hard, but it isn't cruel. It's simply the way life is. Whatever is made is eventually unmade and then remade again.

The shard nestled into Carla's palm like an angular shadow. The black finish of the pottery was set off by white lines. The geometries looked random now, but the whole pot would have revealed patterns that were only hinted at in the shard.

And that, too, was what Luke had told Carla. Then he had held her while she wept and finally accepted that her parents were gone and would never come back again.

For a moment, echoes of past tears ached in Carla's throat. Very carefully she replaced the shard in its velvet-lined nest. Looking back, she knew it had begun then, the years of incoherent longings that had condensed into puppy love, first love, a girl's stumbling progress toward womanhood; it had begun with the ancient pot shard and culminated in an emotion that was as much a part of Carla as breath itself.

As the truth sank into Carla, she measured the depth of the mistake she had made in coming back to the Rocking M; there was no schoolgirl infatuation to be exorcised by a summer's proximity to the everyday reality of Luke MacKenzie. She loved Luke with a woman's timeless, unbounded love. She could more easily sever her right hand from her wrist than she could cut Luke from her soul.

With trembling fingers Carla set the small box back onto the dresser. Just as she turned away, the downstairs telephone rang. She grabbed her robe and raced out of the bedroom.

"Hello?"

"Caught you sleeping, didn't I?" Cash asked.

"Nope. I've become a card-carrying member of the Dawn Brigade since I came to the Rocking M."

Cash laughed. "Well, go back to bed, little sister. I won't be out to pick you up until late afternoon."

"Why?"

"The Jeep is on strike."

"What happened?"

"Who knows?"

"You needn't sound so cheerful about it."

"Sorry, sis. I'll do my best to get out there by four o'clock."

"But it will be too late to go to September Canyon by then and rain showers are predicted tonight and if we aren't on the other side of Picture Wash before it fills it may be days before we can cross!"

"I'm sorry, Carla. Look, maybe I can borrow a truck and—"

"No," she interrupted, feeling guilty for jumping on Cash for something that was beyond his control. "It's all right. I've just been looking forward to seeing September Canyon after all these years of hearing about it."

"Why don't you get Luke to drive you over? He needs a few days off."

The thought of having Luke to herself within the cliff-rimmed silence of the canyon was enough to make Carla's pulse ragged. Yet in the next instant her heartbeat settled to normal, because she knew Luke would refuse to go with her. She had asked him several times to take her to September Canyon; each time he had said no, it was too far to go for just an hour or two of looking around.

"Luke is pretty busy," Carla said neutrally. "If nothing else works out, I'll just drive on ahead. Luke has told me that the canyon isn't hard to find, it's just remote. You can catch up with me when you get your malevolent Jeep straightened out."

There was a silence during which Carla sensed her brother's reluctance to agree to her going to September Canyon without him.

"Promise you won't try rock climbing alone?" he asked at last.

"Of course not. I won't sleep in dry washes during a thunderstorm, either," she added sardonically.

"And if you find any ruins, you won't poke around in them unless someone else is with you?"

"Cash—" she began.

"Promise me, Carla. From what I've heard, some of the floors in those ruins are damned risky."

She sighed. "Cash, I'm twenty-one. I won't do anything foolish, but I won't be hamstrung, either. I've wanted to see September Canyon for seven years. I've worked for weeks and weeks with only a handful of days off in order to save up time. I'm going camping with or without you. If that upsets you, I'm sorry. You'll simply have to trust me."

"What if the Jeep can't be fixed or the rains come and you're stranded in the canyon for a week?"

"I have enough supplies for me for two weeks, remember? I'm carrying your food, too."

"What if it snows?"

"In *August*?" Carla laughed. "C'mon, big brother, you can do better than that. At this time of year I'm far more likely to get sunstroke than frostbite and you know it."

Unwillingly, Cash chuckled. "All right, all right. Let me put it this way, sis. My head knows you're old enough and smart enough to take care of yourself. My gut keeps telling me to protect you."

"Give your gut a rest. Your head did a find job of teaching me how to camp in wild places."

"Won't you be afraid to be alone?"

"Would you?" she asked quickly.

Cash sighed. There was silence for a moment before he said softly, "Okay. I'll catch up with you as soon as I can."

"Thanks, Cash."

"For what?" he muttered. "You would have gone anyway, whether I liked it or not."

"Yes, but thanks for trusting me anyway."

"You're a big girl, Carla. It just takes a little getting used to. Give yourself a hug for me."

"You, too."

Smiling, Carla hung up the phone. The smile faded as she acknowledged to herself the real reason she was going on to September Canyon alone; she was afraid if she stayed at the ranch house one more night, she would say something she would spend the rest of her life regretting.

Something like *I love you, Luke.*

Thirty minutes later Carla had washed, dressed, eaten breakfast and was looking for a good place to leave her note explaining what had happened to Cash's perverse Jeep. Finally she taped the note to the kitchen faucet, knowing that the first thing Luke did at the end of a day was to wash up for dinner.

"I'm coming, damn it!" Luke muttered to the imperiously ringing phone.

Luke told himself that he had come back to the ranch house early to see if Carla had made coffee before she and Cash left, but he knew it was a lie. He was coming in to see Carla before she left—and he was too late, or the damned phone wouldn't be ringing. The kitchen's screen door slammed behind Luke as he strode angrily across the room toward the phone, which had been ringing relentlessly. Fourteen times, by last count.

The lack of savory odors and edible tidbits struck Luke forcefully as he reached for the phone. Without Carla, the kitchen was about as welcoming as the corral trough on a winter morning.

Get used to it, cowboy, he advised himself. *And not for the few days she's camping. A few weeks from now the bet ends.*

Angrily Luke picked up the receiver and snarled, "What!"

Cash whistled softly. "Who bucked you off into the manure pile?"

"Cash? What the hell are you doing near a phone?" Luke demanded. "You and Carla are supposed to be hammering down stakes in September Canyon about now."

"Tell it to my psychotic Jeep."

"Hell," sighed Luke. "How far did you get?"

"Boulder."

"Told you to trade that damned Jeep for a dog and shoot the dog, didn't I?"

"Many times."

Luke laughed shortly. "I'll bet Carla's happy. You've given her a perfect excuse to take off for the brightlights."

"I did?"

"Sure. She's going to see you," Luke said, feeling disappointed that Carla had gone to the city after all.

"She is?"

"Of course she is. She hasn't admitted it to anyone, but I know she's dying to get her hair fixed or her nails done or shop for makeup or whatever it is that women do in big cities."

"We must have a bad connection," Cash said dryly. "Would it help if I banged the receiver on the table?"

"What in hell are you talking about?"

"Funny, I was going to ask you the same question. Let's start all over again. You remember Carla, my kid sister, the one who's been cooking for you and that bunch of starving cowboys since June?"

Luke made a rough sound, but before he could get a word in, Cash kept on going, answering his own question.

"I thought you might. Now Carla—my kid sister, remember?—has been saving up days off so she can go camping in September Canyon. You with me so far?"

"Cash, what the hell—"

"Good," Cash interrupted. "You're still with me. Now hang on tight, cowboy, this is where you got bucked off last time. I am in Boulder. Carla is not. She's not coming here, either. She's on her way to September Canyon."

"Alone?"

"Yes."

"For the love of God, why did you let her do a damn fool thing like that!"

"Yo, Luke!" Cash said loudly. "I think you've been bucked off into the fresh stuff again. Carla, my kid sister—you *do* remember her, don't you?"

Luke swore.

"Yeah, I thought you did," Cash continued. "Well, she's twenty-one. Even if I were at the ranch—which I'm not, remember?—I wouldn't have stopped Carla. She may be my kid sister, but she's not a kid anymore. She's old enough to do what she wants."

Luke started to speak, but Cash wasn't finished talking yet.

"You got that, Luke? Carla's only a girl in our memories, and that's not fair to her or to us. Now, are you still with me or are you sitting on your butt in a pile of road apples wondering what hit you?"

There was silence while Luke absorbed his friend's message. "You're a fool, Cash McQueen," he said softly.

"No. I'm a gambler, which is a different thing entirely. Even so, I'd prefer not to have Carla spending too much time alone in the kind of country she's headed for."

"How long do you think it will take you to get your damned Jeep fixed?" Luke asked tightly.

"I'm having a part flown in from L.A. Soon as that comes I'll be up and running."

"Cash, damn it—"

"Have a nice trip, Luke."

For a long minute Luke stared at the dead phone. Then he slammed the receiver into the cradle and went looking for his ramrod.

~~~~~~~~~

12

Carla's small pickup truck bounced and slithered through one of the countless small washes that crossed the ragged dirt road. When she came to what could have been another ranch crossroad or simply one more "shortcut" leading to nowhere in particular, she stopped the truck and checked the map. Only the dashed, meandering line of the ranch road showed. No crossroads, no spurs, nothing but the single road heading generally southeast across the national forest land where the Rocking M had leased grazing rights. The tongue of national forest ended at the edge of a long line of broken cliffs that zigzagged over the countryside for mile after mile. The line of cliffs was deeply eroded by finger canyons and a few larger canyons where water flowed year-round.

One of those many creases in the countryside was September Canyon.

A swift check of the compass assured Carla that

she was still heading in the right general direction. Out here, that was as good as it got; road signs simply didn't exist. She got out of the pickup, stretched and assessed the weather. Scattered showers had been predicted for the Four Corners country, with a good chance of a real rain by sundown. At the moment clouds were sailing in fat armadas through the radiant sapphire sky. The clouds themselves ranged from brilliantly white to a brooding slate blue that spoke silently of coming rain.

The high peaks off to the north were already swathed in clouds as solitary rainstorms paid court to mountaintops rarely reached by man. To the south, cloud shadows swept over land broken by canyons and rocky ridges. Random, isolated thundershowers showed as thick columns of gray that were embedded in the earth at one end and crowned by seething white billows on the other.

Even as Carla appreciated the splendor of rainbows glittering among the racing storm cells, she was relieved to see that none of the isolated thundershowers had ganged up and settled in anywhere for a good cry. She had driven dirt roads long enough to know that she didn't want to drive through mud if she could help it. Nor was she enthusiastic about the idea of fording washes that were hub-deep in roiling water. Fortunately it was only a few more miles to Picture Wash, and from there it was just under three miles to the mouth of September Canyon. Even if she had to walk, she would have no trouble making it before sunset.

Smiling at the excitement she felt rising in herself at the knowledge that she was finally within reach of the canyon that had haunted her for seven years, Carla got back in her little pickup and drove down the road, trailing a modest plume of dust behind.

The dust Luke raised heading for September Canyon could in no way be called modest. A great rooster tail of grit and small pebbles boiled up in the wake of his full-size pickup truck. He drove hard and fast, but never dangerously. He knew each rut, pothole and outcropping of rock in the road. Close to the ranch house he drove between barbed wire fences marking off pastures. Farther from the house he came to the open grazing land.

There was no gate to the open area. There was only a cattle guard made of parallel rows of pipes sunk into the road at a right angle. The pipes were spaced so that a cow would shy back from walking on them for fear of getting a hoof caught in the open spaces between the bars. The cattle guard offered no deterrent to vehicles beyond the startling noise caused by tires rattling and clattering over pipes.

Luke occupied his mind with the condition of the road or the look of the cattle grazing nearby or the number and kind of plants growing in roadside ditches. The road needed grading. The fences could have used tightening in a few places. The cattle were sleek and serene, grazing in good forage or lying beneath scattered trees to ruminate. The roadside plants were lush with water from a recent storm that had raced by, grooming the land with a wet, lightning-spiked tongue.

More rain threatened. Luke had outrun one thunderstorm, dodged another by taking a shortcut and had plowed through a third. The clouds overhead suggested that evasive maneuvers wouldn't work much longer. He assessed the state of the sky with an anger he didn't examine and pushed harder on the accelerator, picking up speed. If it kept raining off to the southwest, water would be running in Picture Wash before sunset and Carla might become isolated on the other side. There were no other roads into September Canyon. The only trail was one he had discovered seven years before, when he had been combing the Rocking M's most distant canyons on horseback, looking for strays. In good weather the trail was harsh enough; in bad weather it would be hell.

I'll take the trail, if it comes to that. Carla shouldn't be out there by herself.

Why not? asked a sardonic corner of Luke's mind. *She's safer out there alone than she is with me and I damned well know it.*

Surely I can keep my hands off her until Cash gets here.

Yeah, that's what he was gambling on, wasn't it? And that's why I called him a fool.

Luke's mouth flattened into a grim line as the

truck began to descend in a long series of switchbacks that would eventually lead to the lower elevations where Rocking M cattle grazed in winter and cottonwoods grew year-round, shading sand-bottom creeks with massive elegance.

Usually the creeks ran clear, as transparent as the raindrops that had spawned them. But by the time Luke reached Picture Wash, the water was a churning swath of brown. He stopped the truck, got out and guessed the height of the water over the dirt road by how much of the streamside vegetation was underwater. There was no doubt that Carla had crossed here—the narrow tires of her baby pickup had left a trail right into the water. The fact that she hadn't bogged down proved that she had crossed earlier, before Picture Wash had filled with runoff water. The stream was double its normal volume now but still could be forded by a vehicle with four-wheel drive, good axle clearance and a skilled driver. But if Luke had been an hour later, he would have spent the night camped on the wrong side of the wash.

Luke drove the truck through the muddy water and accelerated up the rise on the far side. A passing thunderstorm had dampened the road enough to show tracks clearly but not enough to make driving tricky. The sight of the tread marks left by Carla's ridiculous pickup acted as both goad and lure to Luke. He didn't even pause to look at the outcropping of smooth, rust-colored rock that had given the wash its name. Ancient tribes and not-so-ancient cowboys had inscribed their marks in ageless stone, leaving behind stylized pictographs or impenetrable scrawls.

The road bent off to the right, following the base of the cliffs that paralleled Picture Wash. A few miles farther up, the road turned off into one of the many side canyons that emptied into the wide, sandy wash. There was nothing to mark this canyon as different from any other except the new tire tracks overlying a vague hint of older tracks—that and a discreetly placed cairn of stones telling anyone who could read trail signs to turn left there.

It was barely half an hour to sundown when Luke drove up next to Carla's toy pickup and parked. He got out, took one look at the sky and pulled on a knee-length yellow slicker that was slit up the back to permit riding a horse. Within moments he was headed for the spot where a bend in September Creek had undercut the stone cliff. The creek had long since changed course, cutting a new bed on the far side of the canyon, a hundred yards away and thirty feet lower in elevation. The ancient streambed was now high and dry, protected by an overhang of massive stone that shed rain in long silver veils. Beneath the overhang it was dry except for a single, moss-lined seep no bigger than a hat. The water from the seep was clean and cool and sweet, as heady to a thirsty hiker as wine.

Like the experienced camper she was, Carla had

set everything out before she went exploring. Two sleeping bags were stretched over individual strips of foam mattress. A campfire was laid out, ready to ignite with a single match. Cooking gear and firewood were stacked nearby. Someone who came in cold, wet and tired could be comfortable within a few minutes.

Luke turned his back on the overhang and went looking for Carla. Beyond the protection of the slanting stone, her tracks showed clearly against the countless dimples raindrops had left in the dust. Even though her tracks were obvious, Carla had left a small pile of stones that indicated the direction she had taken. Luke followed quickly, knowing that she would mark any changes in direction by another pile of stones.

Ten minutes later he climbed up the shoulder of a tongue of land that poked out into September Canyon. From where he stood, he couldn't see the overhang where Carla had set up camp, but he could see three miles down the creek itself to the point where it joined Picture Wash. The view was wild, untouched, unchanged since man had first come to walk the land thousands upon thousands of years ago. Indigo storm clouds seethed in slow motion, impaled on shafts of pure light thrown off by the setting sun. Red cliffs wept streams of silver tears, fragile waterfalls whose lifespan could be measured in hours. There was no wind, no rain, no sound but that of silence itself, an immensity that embraced sky and untamed land alike.

And watching it all was Carla, standing at the very edge of the rise, a smile on her lips and serenity in every line of her body.

Slowly Luke walked toward Carla, watching her watch the land, hungry for her in ways he couldn't name, savoring the fact that she so obviously loved the untouched vista of stone and sunlight, silence and cloud. She had had every excuse in the world to drive into Boulder's concrete excitements and enticements, but instead she had headed even deeper into the uninhabited land.

But only for a few days, Luke told himself savagely. *Remember that. She just came here for a few days of vacation. That's a hell of a long way from being able to take a lifetime of isolation. No woman wants that, and no man has the right to ask for that kind of sacrifice.*

And no matter how beautiful the Rocking M might be, it was isolated. There was no doubt about it, no finessing it, no forgetting it.

"You're damn lucky it's me rather than some stranger following your tracks up here," Luke said roughly.

Carla spun around, her eyes wide with surprise. "Luke! My God, you scared me sneaking up like that!"

"Sneaking?" Luke looked at his cowboy boots.

"Schoolgirl, I couldn't sneak up on a corpse wearing these."

"Maybe not, but you crept up on me just fine. What are you doing here?"

"You took the words right out of my mouth."

"I'm taking a vacation, just like I planned."

"Not quite," Luke said tightly. "Last I heard, Cash was still in Boulder."

"Only until the Jeep gets fixed."

"And meanwhile you expected me to let you stay out here alone?"

"Why not? You do several times a year. Cash has more than once."

"That's different."

"It sure is," Carla agreed. "Neither one of you can cook worth a damn. It's a wonder you haven't starved to death. I won't have that problem. I can cook."

"Carla, damn it—" Luke took off his hat and raked his fingers through his hair in frustration.

"What?" she asked calmly.

He hung on to his temper. Barely. "Listen, schoolgirl, this may be a joke to you but it isn't to me. What would you do if you got injured while you were all alone up here?"

"The same thing you or Cash would," Carla said matter-of-factly. "I'd treat myself as best I could and then drive out. If I couldn't drive, I'd make the best shelter I could and wait for someone to miss me, follow my trail markers and help me."

"What if we weren't in time?"

"What if there were a blizzard and I froze to death?" she countered.

"In *August*?"

Carla laughed. "That's exactly what I said to Cash when he dragged up a blizzard as an excuse for me not to come here alone."

Luke snapped his Stetson against his thigh in taut anger. He closed the distance between himself and Carla, not stopping until he was only inches from her.

"What if some man found you here alone?" Luke demanded in a low, hard voice.

"That's less likely to be a problem here than in so-called civilization," Carla pointed out, warily measuring Luke's anger. "In cities women are mugged, beaten or worse. Having other people around is no guarantee a woman is safe from a man."

The sudden wariness in Carla's eyes cost Luke what small hold he had on his tongue. For an instant all he could see was the Carla of three years ago, a girl scared and trembling as his fingers bit into her resilient hips, pulling her close, dragging her up against his hardened body.

"Don't get scared and bolt, schoolgirl," he said coldly. "I won't attack you."

Carla's head came up proudly. "I never thought you would."

"You must have thought it once," he shot back,

"because you ran like hell and stayed away for three years."

With a tight motion of her body, Carla turned away, looking back over the land once more.

"That was humiliation, not fear," she said finally. "I was naive enough to believe I had something to offer you. You pointed out my foolishness in very unmistakable terms. I was mortified, but you had every right to say what you did and I knew it. That's why I was so ashamed."

Luke looked at Carla for a long moment. His mouth flattened in a line of anger and pain. When he spoke, his voice was resonant with restrained emotion.

"I've regretted that night like I've regretted nothing else in my life."

Carla turned back toward Luke, a wondering kind of surprise showing clearly in her blue-green eyes. He was looking at the sky, not at her.

"Rain coming on," he said, replacing his Stetson with a smooth motion. "We'd better get back to camp."

Her thoughts in turmoil, Carla followed Luke back to camp. There was little conversation while she cooked dinner and even less talk while Luke helped her wash dishes. She poured coffee while he added wood to the campfire, increasing the delicate, searing dance of flames. When she handed him a cup of coffee, he thanked her with a nod and then turned his back to the fire and to her, concentrating on the view of September Canyon.

During supper, the last of the red light had drained from the sky, leaving a luminous indigo twilight. Isolated clouds had expanded, flowed outward and joined with others of their kind in a slow embrace. In the darkness soft rain began to condense.

There was no dazzling flare of nearby lightning or fanfare of thunder, simply the gentle persistence of water drops materializing from the night and free-falling through darkness until they caressed the rugged body of the land. Gradually the vast silence became alive with the whispers and sighs and fragmented murmurings of tiny waterfalls gliding over massive stone cliffs.

Carla sat cross-legged near the campfire, looking across the flames at Luke. His yellow slicker had been cast aside beneath the protective overhang. His open-necked shirt, worn jeans and boots were first revealed and then concealed by the languid rise and fall of flames. The metal camp cup he held in his large hand gleamed like quicksilver. He reminded her of the land itself, enduring and powerful, full of unexpected beauty and deep silences.

Luke didn't notice the intensity of Carla's regard. Standing with his back to the flames, he watched the veils of raindrops glittering with reflected fire against the limitless backdrop of night. From time to time he sipped coffee from his cup. Other than that, he made no movement. He neither spoke to nor looked at Carla, yet the silence wasn't uncomfortable, merely an extension of the shared silences they often enjoyed while he ate a late dinner or helped her clean the big coffeepot and measure out coffee for the following morning.

"Why?" Carla asked without warning, as though only seconds had intervened since Luke had stood with her and looked out over the late afternoon on the promontory half a mile up September Canyon.

Not turning around, Luke answered in the same way. "Why did I grab you three years ago?" He laughed roughly. "Hell, schoolgirl, you're not *that* naive."

"And I'm not a schoolgirl anymore. Didn't Cash tell you? I went to college year-round so I could graduate in three years."

Luke said nothing.

Carla persisted, unable to help herself, needing to know about the night that had changed her life, the night that apparently had scarred Luke, too. "Why do you regret what happened so much?"

For a long time there was only silence and the sinuous dance of fire and rain.

"It was the sweetest offer I've ever had," Luke said finally. "You deserved better for it than I gave you. You deserved slow dancing and candlelight kisses and candy wrapped in fancy foil. You deserved a gentle refusal or a gentle lover, and you got...me."

Carla was too surprised to speak. She watched

Luke's shoulders move in what could have been a shrug or the unconscious motion of a man readjusting a heavy burden.

"There was nothing gentle or civilized in me that night. I wanted you until I shook with it. I'd wanted you like that for years. When you seemed to want me, I lost my head."

Luke turned, snapped his wrist and sent the dregs of his coffee hissing into the fire.

"It's just as well," he continued. "Once I was sober I'd have hated myself for taking you. You were so damned innocent. It was better that some other man got to be your first lover. At least he didn't hurt you."

"What?"

Again Luke laughed roughly as he bent over the coffeepot, refilling his cup while he talked. "If your lover had hurt you, it would have made the front pages—'Cash McQueen Avenges Kid Sister.' But there weren't any headlines."

"Not surprising. There wasn't any lover, either."

Luke's head snapped up. For the first time since they had come to camp he looked directly at Carla. Firelight outlined his shocked expression.

"Are you saying that you're...that you haven't...?"

"You needn't look at me like I just fell out of a passing UFO," Carla said uncomfortably. "Has it ever occurred to you that all the studies saying half or two-thirds of girls have lovers before they're married also means that between one-third and one-half of the girls *don't*? What's so shocking about that?''

"One-third of you are saving yourselves for marriage, is that it?'' Luke asked as he set aside the coffeepot and straightened up again.

Carla shrugged, but Luke didn't notice. He had turned his back to the fire again—and to her.

"I don't know what their reason for waiting is,'' Carla said. "I only know mine.''

Silence, a sip of coffee, then Luke asked slowly, "What's your reason?''

"The flame isn't worth the candle.''

"What?''

"More pain than gain,'' Carla said succinctly. "You see, the older I get, the more I realize that I don't like men being close to me. Not like that. Breathing their breath. Tasting them. Not able to move without touching them. *Close*.''

Slowly, as though pulled against his will, Luke turned around to face Carla again. He looked at her for a long, taut moment before he said, "You had a funny way of showing it that night in the dining room when you gave me the sweetest dessert a man ever had.''

The memory of those few, incredible moments in Luke's arms went through Carla like lightning. She tried to speak but was afraid to trust her voice. She licked her lips, looked away from him and tried again to talk.

"It's different with you,'' she said huskily. "It

always has been. I can't…help it. That's just how it is.''

Although Carla tried to speak casually, her voice trembled. The honesty of her words hadn't come without cost; but then, neither had Luke's confession that it had been desire rather than contempt for her that had driven him three years ago.

Abruptly Luke turned away and began prowling the perimeter of the overhang as though he were a cougar measuring the dimensions of its captivity. Half a creature of fire, half a creature of night, wrapped in the elemental rhythms of rain, Luke was a figure born from Carla's dreams. Unable to look away from his lithe, powerful, restless movements, she simply sat and watched him with a soul-deep hunger she couldn't disguise.

And then he turned and looked at her with a hunger as deep as her own.

13

Slowly Carla came to her feet. Without looking away from Luke she skirted the fire, scarcely aware of the flames, for it was the golden blaze of Luke's eyes that consumed her. Motionless, waiting, every muscle taut with his inner struggle, he watched her slow approach. He knew he should turn away from her, walk out into the rain and keep on walking until the heavy running of his blood slowed. He shouldn't stay rooted to the land while she came closer to him. He shouldn't watch with eyes narrowed against the pain of wanting and his whole body rigid from battling his endless hunger for the girl who could arouse him with a word, a look, a breath.

The girl he had promised himself he would never take.

Carla stopped only inches away from Luke. She looked into his eyes until she could bear no more. She leaned forward, speaking his name in a voice as murmurous as the rain. When there was no answer, she raised a trembling hand to his cheek. The gentle touch of her fingers made him shudder as though he had been brushed by lightning. She felt the violent currents of restraint and passion coursing through him as though they were her own. She knew if she touched him again there would be no more turning back for either of them, no more frustrated desire, nothing but the sweeping reality of a man's hunger and a woman's answering love.

Where once the depth of Luke's passion had frightened Carla, it now sent wild splinters of sensation through her. She had never felt the sweet violence of her own sensuality with any other man. She doubted that she ever would—not like this, her body shaking as she reached toward the man she had loved before she understood what a man needed from a woman who loved him.

Delicate fingertips traced Luke's dark eyebrows, the blunt Slavic thrust of his cheekbones, the knife straightness of his nose, the heavy bone of his jaw, caressing him as she had a thousand times in her dreams. When she touched his mouth he made a raw sound and she trembled. That, too, had been part of her dream, his wanting her until he would feel the same tearing pain at not having her that she felt at being separate from him.

"Love me," Carla breathed against Luke's mouth. "Teach me how to love you."

"Baby," Luke said hoarsely, shuddering, unable

to force himself to step back from her. "Don't do this to me. I've wanted you too long."

"Please, Luke. Oh, please, don't turn away. I've dreamed of you for so many years."

Luke looked down at Carla's haunted eyes and trembling lips and suddenly knew that he could no more turn away from her now than he could walk out on his own skin. With that bittersweet realization an odd calm swept through him, a feeling of potency and certainty combined. In no longer battling himself he had redoubled his own strength. That was good. He wanted that extra control. For Carla, not for himself. For Carla he wanted to be the kind of lover he had never been with any woman.

A small movement of Luke's wrist sent his coffee cup in an arc that ended out in the rain. Slowly his big hands came up and framed Carla's face with a tenderness that stopped her breath. Only in that instant did she admit to herself that she had been expecting a passionate onslaught from Luke of the kind that had frightened her three years ago.

"I've dreamed, too," Luke said, his voice deep, watching Carla with eyes that reflected the warmth and heat of flames. "I've filled so many empty hours dreaming of living that night all over again, of having you stand in front of me again, offering yourself, looking at me and trembling with hope and desire. And now you're standing in front of me again, and you're trembling... Is it fear, sunshine? Tell me it isn't fear."

"I don't know why you make me shake," Carla said, trying to laugh, making only an odd, ragged sound. "But I know it isn't fear."

Luke's slow, essentially male smile made Carla's heart turn over with desire. The leashed hunger in his eyes stopped her breath. Gently he turned her until her back was no longer to the fire. Without moving, hardly even breathing, he looked for a long time at the silken curves of her hair, the elegant arch of her eyebrows and the silent dance of flames reflected in her eyes. And then he began looking at her all over again.

She didn't understand why he had turned her profile to the fire, why he made no move to touch her now. "L-Luke?"

"I want to see you," he said simply. "I want you to see me."

The warmth of his hands enveloped Carla in a gentle vise. His lips traced the graceful margin between her hair and her face, smoothed her eyebrows, breathed warmth against her eyelids, outlined the hollow of her cheeks, whispered along her chin. She stood enthralled, unable to move even if she had wanted to, unable even to breathe, suspended between fire and rain and the unexpected, exquisite tenderness of Luke's passion. When his lips finally brushed her mouth, her pent breath came out in a moan.

Luke froze, lifted his head and saw the glitter of tears caught in Carla's long lashes.

"Does my kiss really mean that much to you?" he asked, his voice strained.

She opened her eyes and looked at him, unable to speak.

"My God," he whispered, shaken.

He bent down to her mouth once more, murmuring the nickname he had given to her the first time he had seen her smile so many years ago. The sound of his voice mixed with the fluid murmur of water sliding over stone in the darkness beyond the fire. He brushed her mouth once, twice, then again and again, touching her with the tip of his tongue each time, taking tiny sips of her until her lips parted helplessly, hungrily, and the tip of her tongue touched his.

"Yes," Luke said huskily, encouraging her. "Do you want that, too? Do you want to taste me the way you did in the dining room?"

Blindly Carla turned her face to follow Luke's teasing, gentle, maddening mouth, lips that kissed and lifted, kissed and lifted, never giving her what she suddenly, wildly needed. She made a sound of frustration and need that was too ragged to be a word.

"I hope yes is what you're trying to say, sunshine," he murmured, flexing his hands, pulling her closer to his body. "I hope you liked the taste and feel of me, because remembering that kiss has kept me awake too damned many nights since then."

Carla's eyes opened in surprise. "You, too? I would lie in bed and remember kissing you."

She didn't understand what it did to Luke to hear that hunger for him had left her sleepless. She only knew that the powerful hands framing her face trembled for an instant. He breathed a word that could have been prayer or curse or both hotly mingled.

"Show me the kind of kiss you wanted when you lay awake," Luke said against Carla's lips. "Show me your dreams. Let me make them come true."

Her arms slid up around Luke's neck as she pulled herself up on tiptoe, balancing against his big body. His palms slid from her face to her shoulders and then around her waist, holding her close, but not so close that she would be frightened by the hard bulge of flesh beneath his jeans. Softly her lips brushed his and her tongue glided along his lower lip. He shuddered but made no move to take her mouth. Her arms tightened more and she trembled.

"Please," Carla whispered against his lips. "Please, Luke. In my dreams I tasted you."

Luke's lips opened on a low sound of pleasure-pain and suddenly there was no barrier to the kind of kiss Carla had both remembered and dreamed. Her tongue sought and found his for a wild, hungry tasting; and then his arms closed harshly around her, arching her into his body in helpless response to the naked, innocent demands of her kiss. Instantly he tried to pull back, cursing his own loss of control.

But Luke found he couldn't pull back. An unexpected, fiercely feminine strength held him close, for Carla was placing no leash on her own response, her own dreams. She was kissing him as she had dreamed of being kissed, hunger and trembling, heat and sensual fire; and something more, something she couldn't name but knew waited for her within this one man's arms.

Luke bent down, arching Carla's supple body more deeply, bending her into the curve of his own body, satisfying her instinctive urgency to match a woman's soft heat with a man's hard need. His arms tightened even more as he slowly lifted her until she had no support but his strength, no place to rest but against his hard flesh, nothing but his heat and hunger surrounding her. She was spinning languidly, turning, folded in hot darkness, sweetly consumed by fire, and Luke was spinning with her, the taste of him spreading through her, his arms locked around her, a dream coming true, wrapping her in ribbons of fire.

A long time passed before Carla felt herself being lowered slowly to the ground, still held so close as Luke eased her down his body that she could feel each ripple of his muscles, the snaps of his shirt, the blunt metal of his belt buckle and the much blunter ridge of his arousal pressing against her. When her feet touched the ground she stumbled, taken unaware by the weakness of her knees. Instantly his arms tightened, supporting her. She felt the rock hardness of his thighs and then he groaned, locking her hips against his as he moved in the primal rhythms that had once frightened her and now sent an incandescent heat cascading through her, echoing the movement of his hips.

Groaning, Luke tore his mouth away from Carla's and forced himself to loosen his hold on her. He was breathing roughly, all but out of control. His mouth felt empty, violently hungry for the sultry completion it had so recently known. He closed his eyes, caught between frustration and surprise.

"Luke?" Carla asked shakily. "What is it? Did I do something wrong?"

His eyes opened. Her breath stopped as she looked at the twin pools of molten gold. His smile was like his eyes, hot and restrained, bemused and very hungry.

"It's all right," Luke said. "I just thought I knew all that mattered about men and women and sex. I was wrong."

"What do you mean?"

"I can't put it in words, but I know it's true just the same. Give me your mouth again, sunshine. I've never enjoyed just kissing anyone so much in my life."

"But I'm not—not that experienced," Carla said, perplexed and pleased at once, her thoughts vaporizing at the heat of his eyes, her hands clinging to his arms because she was thoroughly off balance.

Luke's eyelids lowered in reflexive pleasure as he ran his thumb over Carla's flushed lips. She followed his caresses with the tip of her tongue, caressing him in turn.

"You're so damned honest," he said huskily. "Your words, your responses. I didn't know a woman could be that passionately honest. It's making things harder than I expected. Kiss me, baby."

"What things?" Carla said shakily, letting Luke take the weight of her body as she reached up to give him the kiss he had requested. Then she heard her own words and buried her face against his neck, realizing anew precisely what that hard ridge of flesh was beneath his jeans—and aware, too, that his arousal made her feel proud and restless and more than a little curious all at once. "Er, besides the obvious, that is."

"It's obvious, all right." Luke laughed softly, realizing that his changed body didn't frighten Carla as it had three years ago. He tilted her face up and saw the mixture of feminine pride and virginal curiosity in her expression. Amusement and passion warred for control of his body. Both won. "God, I wish I could stop time and keep you locked away forever. My own very private supply of sunshine," he said against her lips.

When Carla started to answer, Luke took her mouth with a hunger that shook both of them. She felt vividly the velvet penetration of his tongue, the power and hardness of his arms lifting her, the world turning and dipping, ribbons of fire wrapping around them once more. When the ground came up softly to meet her, she realized that she was lying on one of the sleeping bags with Luke beside her, urging her closer and closer to himself. She trembled even as she pressed more intimately against his big body.

"Are you all right?" he asked.

"Yes."

"You're trembling."

"So are you."

"I know. I barely had the strength to lift you."

Carla's eyes widened and her hands tightened on Luke's muscular shoulders, silently pointing out the inherent power of his body.

"Yeah, being weak came as a surprise to me, too," he said, his voice uneven with desire and laughter. He whispered her name and bent down to her mouth once more. "I ache, Carla. Want to kiss me and make it all better?"

The passionate whimsy of Luke's question made her smile. She was still smiling when his mouth came down on hers in a slow, complete mating that drew a moan from deep within her. He drank the small sound and thirsted for more.

Luke's hands smoothed over Carla's body, seeking her breasts, caressing them in hot silence. Her cotton shirt and sheer bra didn't conceal her immediate response. He caught the hardened nipple between his fingers and plucked rhythmically, hearing her shattered moan, tasting it, feeling it, demanding it with the deep seduction of his kiss and the hunger of his hands.

When Carla's breasts were hot and swollen, their tips hard and aching for more of Luke's caresses, his right hand slid down her body. Stroking, probing, smoothing, inciting, he savored the curve of her waist and belly. She arched against his hand, burning and shivering, needing something more, unable to tell him what she wanted because her mouth was wholly his, caught in a slow mating she didn't want to end.

Luke's palm caressed her hips and thighs repeatedly, pressing against her, moving her in the rhythms of his tongue deep within her sweet mouth. Gently, inevitably, his hand eased higher and higher between her thighs until he could go no farther. His fingers curved around her and his palm began to move slowly, insistently, rhythmically; and the sultry heat that blossomed at his touch made him groan.

His hands and mouth became harder, more demanding, dragging a broken sound from Carla, a sound that incited Luke unbearably. He wanted to hear more such cries ripple from her, wanted to coax them from her in a fiery, unending cascade, wanted to discover and savor and taste each of her responses. He wanted to consume her and find hot consummation in an unbridled intimacy he had neither sought nor desired with any woman but her, and he wanted it until he died.

The broken whimpers Carla was making finally penetrated Luke's passion. He tore his mouth away from hers and dragged his hands free of her rich, alluring softness.

"Luke—please—I—"

In the moment before control came back to Luke, he shuddered like a man in torment.

"Sorry," he said hoarsely, smoothing the hair away from Carla's face. "I'm sorry, sunshine. I didn't mean to frighten you."

"That's not—" Carla's voice broke. "I didn't mean—"

She tried to bring herself under control but couldn't. She made a ragged sound and captured one of Luke's hands, kissed his palm, then closed her teeth on it in helpless response to the baffling, conflicting feelings raging within her, wanting to caress and savage him at the same time.

"Oh, baby," Luke said, closing his eyes, his whole body clenched in violent response. "You're killing me and you don't even know it."

"I'm sorry," Carla said shakily, shocked by her own actions. "I don't know why I did that. I just—just—"

He didn't wait for her to finish her sentence. "I'll forgive you if you do it again."

"What?"

"You heard me. Only harder, baby. Harder."

Luke's body tightened as Carla sank her teeth into the pad of flesh at the base of his thumb. Her barely restrained violence told Luke that her frustration equaled his own, and she didn't even know what she was missing. The thought of giving her what she needed sent a searing rush of blood through his body that nearly undid him.

Watching Carla, feeling as though he were going to lose control with the next breath or the one after, Luke lifted his hand, licked the small marks she had left on his skin and saw her tremble. His fingers closed on his collar and he pulled sharply. The shirt came undone with a rippling sound as metal snaps gave way, revealing a dark pelt of hair and muscles gleaming with firelight and desire. His hand shot out and wrapped around her head, pulling her against his naked chest.

"Again," Luke whispered.

Uncertain, Carla brushed her mouth over Luke's chest, raked him lightly with her teeth, tasted the salt of his passion and the fierceness of his restraint, inhaled the exciting smell of skin and soap and male heat. Slowly she put her mouth against Luke again, tasted him again, felt the unbridled sensuality of his response. A soft, fragmented sound came from her lips as urgency rushed through her, twisting her, making her ache. Her hands clenched against his chest.

"Harder," Luke said, watching Carla with burning golden eyes. "Go ahead. Bite me. That's what you want. You're shaking and tied up in knots and you know I'm the cause of it and you want it to stop but you want it to go on forever, too. You're frustrated and on fire and confused and you want to take it out on me. Do it, baby. *Do it.*''

With a small, wild cry, Carla did what Luke urged, what she wanted, what she needed. Her teeth sank sensually into the flexed muscles of his chest, testing his strength and her own restraint at the same time. He made a hoarse sound of pleasure and encouragement. Her fingers worked through the wedge of springy, silky hair, pulling and kneading, her nails biting into his hard flesh even as her teeth did.

Luke laughed and urged Carla on while he undressed her. His words were dark and hot, punctuated by the ragged rush of her breathing and his own. The scoring of her nails down his chest was like wild, hot rain, and the primitive caress of her teeth was stroke after stroke of lightning scorching through him, setting him on fire. He didn't know how much longer he could endure the sweet torment, but he knew he was going to find out. The thought of denying himself one fiery instant of Carla's passion was worse than any frustration he might feel at the moment.

With a hoarse groan Luke finally pulled Carla's mouth up to his own and devoured her in a ravenous kiss that would have frightened her only minutes before; but now she needed that fierce claiming more than breath itself. She put her arms around his neck, tangled her fingers deeply in his hair and gave back the kiss with an unleashed passion that matched his.

The world spun again as Luke's hands moved over Carla like hard, warm rain, dissolving everything away, leaving her naked and shivering in his arms. He held her, felt her shaking, heard her broken breaths and remembered all the years he had spent dreaming of having her offer herself to him again and his own vow that he would be gentle if she ever did. Cursing his own nearly overwhelming need, aching, burning alive, he fought for self-control.

Carla called his name, her voice breaking.

"It's all right," Luke said tightly. "I won't hurt you, sunshine. You're so wild that I forgot you're not used to this."

She forced herself to breathe. "C-can you get used to this?"

"Being naked?"

She shook her head. He saw the helpless shivering of her body and waited, but she said nothing more.

"What?" he urged softly.

Carla made an odd sound and dug her nails into Luke's chest in an unconscious gesture of sheer frustration.

"Wanting," she said, her voice aching. "And not having. Wanting and wanting and *wanting*."

Before she had finished speaking, Luke turned away and began stripping off his own clothes, throwing them aside. When he turned back to Carla and lay on his side again, she was sitting up, looking at him. All of him. He froze, motionless, regretting his haste and the fact that she had never seen a naked, aroused man before; and he had never been more aroused. He saw the change in her expression, the heedless passion suddenly checked, as though the blunt reality of his hunger had shocked her.

"Still want me?" Luke asked, his voice rough with restraint.

Carla's only answer was the glide of her fingernails over Luke's chest, down the center line of his body, below his navel to the thatch of dark hair. There she hesitated for a moment before she touched the evidence of his desire with curious fingertips. When he jerked reflexively, she looked up into his blazing golden eyes.

"I don't know which is more exciting," he said thickly, "seeing your sweet curiosity or feeling it."

"You don't...mind?"

Slowly Luke shook his head, then caught his breath as Carla's soft fingertips found each irregularity in his hot flesh and lovingly traced it. He had never known such a fragile, tender, consuming exploration. He had never guessed that he could be so aroused without losing control, but he refused to consider letting go, because even in sexual release he had never known such wild pleasure as he was discovering right now.

"Will you mind?" Luke asked, running his hand caressingly along Carla's calf, her knee, her inner thigh.

"What?"

"When I touch you the way you're touching me."

Before Carla could answer, his fingers had discovered the soft, swollen, sultry flesh at the apex of her thighs. She made a startled sound and reflexively closed her legs around his hand.

"Is that yes or no?" Luke asked, rubbing gently, finding and stroking the nub hidden within her soft folds.

Carla's breath broke as pleasure showered through her, a wild, unexpected cascade of sensation that made her shudder. He felt the sudden, small melting, saw mist bloom beneath the firelight on her skin and wanted to lower himself over her, sink into her, filling her, bathing his aching flesh in her passionate response. Eyes closed, back arched, moving helplessly against his touch, she shivered again, melted again, searing him with her heat.

"Sunshine?" Luke whispered, caressing Carla with tiny motions, tearing a moan from her lips. "Look at me."

Carla's eyes opened, dazed by passion. His hand moved again, sliding over her, gilding her with the sultry rain of her own response. He wanted more, much more of her, but he didn't want to take it. He wanted her to give herself to him while she looked at him, knowing every bit of what was happening.

"Don't hide, baby," he said softly. "Open for me."

For a moment Carla looked at Luke; then his fingertips moved gently and pleasure shimmered and burst inside her. With a small moan she shifted her legs, allowing him greater intimacy, wanting it as much as he did.

"That's it," he said, his low voice both praising and encouraging her. "Brace yourself on your hands and relax those beautiful legs for me."

As Carla leaned back, Luke's fingers moved coaxingly, skimming her flushed skin, teasing her, asking silently for what she had given no other man.

"L-Luke?"

"It's all right," he said, his voice deep. "Just a little more. Open just a little more. Let me—" His voice broke as Carla obeyed, allowing him into her softness. "Oh, baby, you're like honey."

He shuddered even as she did, pleasure rushing wildly between them at the slow glide of his caress, penetration and retreat, a silken measuring of her ability to receive the gift of his body. Slowly he rose over her, kneeling between her legs, redoubling and deepening his presence within her softness. When his thumb found and teased the velvet focus of her passion, she sank back onto the sleeping bag with a hoarse cry.

Luke froze, afraid that he had hurt Carla despite all his care.

"Don't stop," she pleaded brokenly, looking at him, moving helplessly against his hand, caught up in an urgency that stripped away everything but her incandescent need. "Oh, Luke, if you stop I'll die."

"Sunshine," he said, "baby, are you sure?"

Carla's body answered for her, bathing Luke in sweet fire, burning away all his questions. Slowly he lowered himself over her. The teasing of his fingertips was replaced by the hard flesh she had so recently explored. The satin caress sent ripples of pleasure through her, expanding rings of sensation that burst sweetly, melting her in rhythmic waves. Gently Luke rode the waves of her passion, letting them ease his way, merging with her gradually, lovingly.

The slow consummation wrung a low moan from Carla. She had never felt anything so exquisite as the merging of flesh with flesh, the elemental fire of her lover's body blending with her own equally elemental rain. A lightning stroke of pain flashed through her, but it swirled away and was lost in the glittering, gathering storm that was consuming her—Luke's mouth on her neck, her throat, her eyelids, and his fiery words licking over her. She arched upward again and again in the primal rhythm of the union. His body enfolded her, surged deeply within her, a part of her. She tried to tell him that she could take no more, the pleasure was too great, she was dying; but the only word she could say was his name. A glittering darkness swept over her, followed by a wild shimmering of her body that shook her to her soul, hurling her into ecstasy.

Luke heard his own name called again and again, a passionate litany that echoed the rhythmic tightening of Carla's body beneath him, around him, demanding all that he had withheld, all that he was, all that he had. Her name was a hoarse cry torn from his throat as passion exploded into a release that was unlike any he had ever known, violent and tender at once, ecstasy convulsing him savagely, softly, endlessly, as he gave himself to the woman he had sworn never to take.

14

Carla stirred and reached out for the muscular warmth she had become accustomed to during the night. When her hands found nothing but cool air and emptiness rather than Luke's big body, her eyes opened. An instant later she saw him. Wearing only jeans, he was standing at the edge of the overhang, sipping coffee, watching a land swept clean by rain. As though he sensed that she had awakened, he turned around. The hot cascade of sunlight pouring in behind him made it impossible for her to see the expression on his face.

Without a word Luke came and sat on his heels next to Carla's sleeping bag. Light illuminated half his face, leaving the other half in darkness. For long moments he watched Carla with tawny, enigmatic eyes. Cradled between his hands, the metal camp cup sent fragrant steam into the air.

"Are you all right?" he asked finally.

She nodded and slid her hand from the sleeping

bag's warmth to touch the smoothness of Luke's freshly shaved cheek.

He closed his eyes. "Are you sure?"

"Luke, what's wrong?"

"When I washed this morning…" His voice faded. "You bled last night."

"It didn't hurt then. Or now."

Luke said something rough underneath his breath and stood up with an abrupt surge of power. *"You were a virgin."*

"You knew that before you—before we—" Carla stammered. "Luke, I told you. You knew!"

"Yes," he said savagely. "I knew. But I didn't really *know* until I saw your blood on my body this morning. Then it all became real. Too real." He raked his fingers through his hair. "God, what a mess!"

Carla felt as though she had been struck. Stunned, she said nothing.

Without looking at her, Luke stalked back to the overhang and stared broodingly out over the uninhabited land.

"Well, schoolgirl, you got what you wanted," Luke said after a moment, sending the dregs of his coffee arcing into the sunshine with a brutal snap of his wrist. "I hope to hell it was worth the price."

"I don't—don't understand."

"No, I don't suppose you do. That's what being young is all about. Doing and not understanding. But I understand. I should have walked away from you. I knew it the same way I know fire is hot and rain is wet." Memories tightened Luke's body, echoes of a passionate night he would never forget. "But I didn't have the strength to walk away from you."

Carla felt cold seeping into her flesh, settling in an icy lump at the pit of her stomach as she remembered what Luke had told her weeks before: *Stay away from me, sunshine. I'm afraid I won't have the strength to say no. Then I would take you and hate you...*

"Get up, Carla. I've got water warmed for you. After you wash we'll go into town and make a bigger mistake than we made last night. But there's no help for that, either."

There was no inflection in Luke's voice, nothing to tell Carla what he was thinking.

"What will be doing in town?" she asked warily.

"Can't you guess, schoolgirl? This is your lucky day. You're getting married."

There was a long silence while Carla measured the hard features of the man she loved.

"Why?" she asked.

Luke made a savage, impatient gesture. "Last night, that's why, and you damned well know it. You came to September Canyon a virgin. No man worth the name would take that from you and give nothing in return."

A slow, complex anger blossomed in Carla. She

had dreamed of marriage to Luke, but never under these circumstances—duty and honor, not love.

He didn't love me years ago. He didn't love me last night. He doesn't love me now.

Nothing has changed.

Then Carla realized that something had changed; she wasn't a child to run from Luke's anger anymore. Nor was she childish enough to cross her fingers, marry a man who didn't love her and hope that it would all work out.

"The rest of your life seems an excessive price for a fast toss," Carla said evenly.

Luke gave her a sharp look but saw only a feminine reflection of his own lack of expression. That surprised him. He had become accustomed to watching moods and emotions move across Carla's face.

"I knew the stakes when I took cards in the game," Luke said curtly, looking away from the elegant feminine curves rising above the sleeping bag's dark green material. "Hurry up and get dressed. If we don't get out of here quick, we might not get out for days. It's already raining in the highlands. Won't be long before it gets wet here."

"Don't let me keep you."

"Your baby pickup won't get one hundred yards the way the road is now. You'll have to come with me. We'll get your truck later."

"No."

"What?"

"No," Carla repeated coolly. "N-o. A word signifying refusal. A negative. The opposite of yes.'' Each syllable was clipped, unflinching. ''I'm not going with you in your truck. I'm not going into town with you. I'm not marrying you. I came to September Canyon for a vacation. I'm going to have that vacation. If you don't like it, you're free to leave.''

Luke's head snapped around. He had never heard that precise tone from Carla, smooth and remote and utterly controlled, telling him that he had no right to order her around.

But she was as wrong as she was naive. He knew what had to be done. ''Listen, schoolgirl—''

''I've listened,'' Carla interrupted, ''which is more than you have. One. I'm not a schoolgirl. Two. You've made it very clear that you don't want to marry me. Three. There will be no marriage.''

''Four,'' he shot back. ''You might be pregnant. Ever think of that, schoolgirl? Or are you on the pill?''

''N.Y.P., cowboy,'' she said with a calmness she didn't feel.

''What does that mean?''

''Not Your Problem.''

''What the hell are you talking about? Of course it's my problem! Or didn't you know that it takes two to make a baby?''

''And only one to carry it. Guess which one of us that is? N.Y.P, cowboy.''

Luke glared at Carla. She didn't back up one inch, giving back a stare as level as his own. He measured her determination and realized that the deep well of passion he had discovered in Carla wasn't limited to making love. The girl who had fled from his passion three years ago had become a woman with cool blue-green eyes and hot flags of anger flying in her cheeks. The combination was…exciting.

Angrily Luke felt his body respond as it had always responded to Carla. His lack of control over himself made him furious.

"What are you planning on telling Cash when you start losing your waistline and your breakfast?" Luke asked coldly.

"*If* that happens—and it is by no means a certainty—I'll tell Cash that he'll be an uncle along about May of next year."

Luke's breath came in swiftly. An odd feeling twisted through him at the thought of Carla having his child.

"After you tell him, Cash will do his best to kill me," Luke pointed out. "Is that what you want? Revenge?"

"Don't worry. I'll make it very clear that I turned down your generous offer of marriage."

"That won't be good enough. He'll want to know why. So try out your so-called reasoning on me. Why won't you marry me?"

"Unlike you, Cash is bright enough to figure out all by himself that I don't want to spend the rest of my life as your jailer."

Luke's breath came in sharply. "Funny you

should put it that way. I sure as hell don't want to spend my life as your jailer, either. And that's how you would come to look at the Rocking M—as a jail.''

"You're wrong. I love the ranch."

"For a few weeks. In the summer. What about in the winter, Carla? What about the day I come back from breaking ice in the watering troughs and find my children sobbing and terrified because their mother is screaming in god-awful harmony with the wind? What then?"

The past haunted Luke's topaz eyes and his deep voice. The sight of his pain took away Carla's anger, leaving only her love. She ached to take the darkness from him, healing him, giving him hope for the future; but she couldn't change the past and she didn't know how to make him believe in their future. In her.

"I'm sorry, Luke. I'm so sorry." Carla's voice thinned with the effort of controlling her tears. "Please believe me. I'd give anything to be able to change your past. Except last night. I wouldn't trade last night, Luke. I have a whole life to live. I want to live it knowing that once, just once, I touched the sun."

Thunder belled through September Canyon, following invisible lightning. The scent of fresh rain drifted beneath the overhang. There was a random pattering, like an orchestra warming up, and then the raindrops gathered and began falling in a gentle, consuming rhythm.

Luke heard the sound and knew it was too late to go into town; but then, it had been too late the instant he had heard her describe the night she had first felt him within her body.

I touched the sun.

The knowledge that being his lover had meant so much to Carla disarmed Luke. He had taken something from her that she could give only once, yet she had no recriminations, no harsh words, no hints of the raw truth: he had been experienced, she had not. He had known where the kisses would inevitably end. She had not. He should have controlled himself.

He had not.

Gently Luke pulled Carla from the folds of the sleeping bag and into his arms. He wanted to tell her that knowing he had pleased her made him feel proud and powerful and oddly humble, but he had no words, nothing to give her in return, nothing to remake the unchangeable instant when elemental need had transformed her, taking virginity and bringing ecstasy in return.

"I'm glad I brought you pleasure," Luke said huskily. "I would take back every instant if I could, but not that. It's so rare, sunshine. So damned rare."

The feel of Carla's warm, bare skin against his body as she put her arms around him made Luke ache with more than sexual need. He held her close, rocking very slowly, smoothing her hair with the palm of his hand, knowing with a combination of sweetness and sadness that she had touched him in a way no other woman had, taking him to the sun, sharing the burning center of life itself with him.

And he could not have her again.

He must not. For her sake, and for his own. He was all wrong for her. She was all wrong for him, a modern woman on a ranch where time stood still, imprisoning women, breaking them. Carla was far too generous and beautiful to be destroyed like that. She deserved more than he had given her. She deserved to be cherished, protected, revered...sunshine in a world that knew too much darkness.

Luke touched Carla's lips with a single brushing kiss before he loosened his arms and led her the few steps to the fire. Without a word he poured part of a bucket of warm water into a washpan, swirled a cloth around, soaped it and handed it to her.

"If you're shy about washing in front of me, I'll take a walk," he said quietly.

Carla's hand was shaking so much the slippery cloth eluded her fingers. Luke caught the warm, soapy cloth and looked questioningly at her.

"Are you sure you're all right?"

"I'm s-sorry," she said, trying to control her voice.

But Carla did no better steadying her voice than she had her hands. She ducked her head, hiding her eyes as she tried to take the cloth from Luke's hand.

He didn't let go. Instead he put his other hand beneath her chin so that she had to meet his eyes.

"Sunshine, what's wrong?"

"Don't you know?"

Helplessly Carla looked at the tempting masculine pelt curling down until it narrowed and vanished beneath the jeans he had pulled on without bothering to button them more than halfway. As she saw the faint crescents and scratches on his skin, memories of last night swept over her. He had been so perfect as a lover and she had been so eager, so breathless, so *inexperienced*. No wonder he wasn't doing handsprings at having her naked in his arms again. She had clawed him like a cat, left marks on him, bitten him, demanding him, all of him.

Carla sucked in her breath, closing her eyes, unable to face Luke with the memory of her own wantonness burning in her mind.

"No, I guess you don't know," Carla said, her tone ashamed and almost bitter. "Why should you? I don't affect you the same way you affect me."

"Look at me," Luke said, his voice deep, gentle, soothing. "Tell me what's wrong."

Carla's eyes opened. She looked through Luke rather than at him.

"In case you hadn't noticed," she said tightly, "I'm stark naked and you're nearly so, and you can make me tremble when you're fully clothed and clear across the room. It was bad enough before last night, but now it's worse. I want you. *I still want you.* And you don't...you don't want..." Her voice frayed.

Blood hammered explosively through Luke, wrenching at his self-control.

"Sweet God," Luke said harshly. "You do know how to push a man, don't you? I promised myself I wouldn't touch you that way again and there you stand naked and shaking. And then you tell me you want me! How the hell am I supposed to say no?"

"I didn't ask you to say no, did I?" Carla laughed unhappily and made a grab for the washcloth. "Never mind, Luke. I don't blame you. In your shoes I don't suppose I'd be dying for another round of amateur hour, either."

The savage word he said made her wince.

"That's not what I meant and you know it," Luke said between clenched teeth. "Damn it, Carla, *help me*. I'm trying not to ruin your life!"

"Of course," she said, her voice sad and empty and utterly disbelieving.

The unhappiness in Carla's face and tone affected Luke as deeply as the passion that was making her tremble.

"Baby, please...don't do this to me."

The yearning, husky timbre of Luke's voice made Carla bite back tears. Automatically she reached out to him in pain and sympathy and a need that transcended even the desire she felt for him. When her fingers touched his chest a visible shudder of response went through him.

"Luke, I—"

"Too late," he interrupted heavily. "It always seems to be too late with you. All you have to do is touch me and I burn. I should say no to you. I know it. But I can't. Give me your mouth, baby. It's a lifetime since I kissed you."

Luke's free hand threaded into the silky curls of Carla's hair, seeking the warmth of her scalp, pulling her head back as he lowered his mouth over hers. His tongue probed her lips until she sighed and he slid into her eager warmth. The kiss was deep, heavy, drenched with the sensuality Luke had spent years trying to control around Carla.

But no longer. The past was as cold as the future would be, but the present was here, now, and it seethed with fire.

When Luke finally ended the kiss, separating himself from Carla, she whimpered softly, wanting more. The sweet sound made him smile, but he didn't take up the flushed invitation of her lips. Keeping his hands off her was impossible, but he would at least control the way he touched her. A few more kisses like that and he would lose his head as he had last night, taking her without protecting her.

"I didn't tell you what it was like for me last night," Luke said, slowly rubbing the soapy cloth over Carla's shoulders, her neck, her arms. "I don't know if I can tell you. I'm damned sure I shouldn't even try, but shouldn't doesn't seem to cut much ice when it comes to you, sunshine.''

Luke's crooked smile tugged at Carla's heart, making her want to smile and cry in return. She started to speak but the words wedged in her throat when the warm cloth moved over her breasts and they tightened in a wild, aching rush.

The sound of the cloth being rinsed out blended with the gently seething rain. After a few moments Luke laid aside the cloth and soaped up his hands instead.

"I barely touched you last night," Luke said. He smiled at Carla's look of shocked disbelief. "It's true, baby. I should have made it last forever. I wanted to, but you made me lose my head. You're making shreds of my control now. Look."

He held up his soapy hands, revealing their fine tremor.

"But I didn't mean to," she said. "I don't even know how to. It's just that when you touch me—"

The words became a moan as his hands found her taut breasts and began smoothing over them in warm, soapy caresses.

"I love hearing your breath break when I touch you," Luke murmured. "I love feeling your breasts rise to meet my hands. I love feeling your nipples harden. I love knowing that your heart is beating faster and your breath—"

Carla tried to speak, but all that came out was a

husky sound of pleasure when his fingers teased her, making her nipples harden even more.

"—your breath is coming faster," he whispered. "I love that, too. I love knowing you're as helpless to control your body when I touch you as I am when you touch me."

The gentle, irresistible tugging of Luke's fingers made a wild shiver course visibly through Carla's body. His eyes narrowed into glittering topaz slits as he felt an answering thrill race through his own flesh. An odd, consuming curiosity bloomed in him as he dipped his hands in warm water and rubbed up a mound of lather before turning back to her.

"Baby?" Luke whispered against Carla's mouth, finding her nipples, tugging at them. "What does it feel like when I do this to you?"

"Like—" She made a breathless sound and lifted herself into his touch, twisting slowly, increasing the pressure of his caress.

"Tell me," he coaxed.

"Fire," she whispered. "A glittering kind of fire going all the way to my knees."

Strong hands followed Carla's words, moving slowly, caressing and bathing her in consuming intimacy. His fingers slid delicately between her legs, bringing pleasure even as they gently washed away all signs that she had given herself to a man for the first time only a handful of hours ago.

For long, wild moments there was only the sound of Carla's ragged moans and Luke's hands gliding over her body and the rain outside softly sliding over hard stone. When Luke knew his control could take no more, he reluctantly turned away, grabbed the washrag with fingers that insisted on trembling, and rinsed the cloth thoroughly. He rinsed Carla just as thoroughly, bringing the clear water to her skin again and again, touching her as impersonally as he could until not a bit of soap remained; and still he rinsed her, for it was his only excuse to touch her.

"Luke?" Carla asked finally, not understanding.

She could see by the tension of his face and the occasional tremor in his hands that he was aroused, yet nothing caressed her except warm water and the soft cloth.

"Hold still, sunshine. I'm almost done."

His voice was deep, husky with the pounding of his blood.

"Does that mean I get to bathe you next?"

The thought of Carla's hands touching him as intimately as he had touched her made Luke groan and swear at the same time. After a final, unnecessary passage of the washcloth over the dark, damp triangle at the apex of Carla's thighs, Luke very delicately ran his fingertip between her legs, smiling and aching at her response.

"Bathing me would be a bad idea," he said hoarsely.

"Why? Wouldn't you like it?"

"I'd like it too much. I'd lose control."

Carla's eyes widened.

"It's always been that way with you," Luke said simply. "I was afraid if I ever touched you, I'd have to fight myself to let you go. The first time I touched you, you ran. If you hadn't, I'd have laid you down in front of the fireplace and taken you. The second time I touched you, you didn't run. I had a hell of a battle with myself, sunshine. Since that night I've dreamed of having you in my lap again, only this time your body would fit me like a hot satin glove…"

Luke's voice frayed. For a few moments there was silence while he visibly fought for self-control.

"So I didn't touch you after that night in the dining room," Luke continued roughly. "Until last night."

"But I wanted you to touch me," Carla whispered. "I wanted it so much I would wake up in the middle of the night and ache. For you, Luke. *For you.*"

The words sent a hammer blow of need through Luke that brought him to his knees. He put his forehead against Carla and fought for control.

"I'm aching so much now," she said huskily. "I hurt. Make the ache go away, Luke."

"Baby…oh, God…don't…"

"Please," Carla whispered, shivering. "Please, Luke. Love me."

Luke's fingers bit painfully into the resilient curves of Carla's hips. He shuddered once, a whiplash of violent need and restraint. Then the grip of his fingers eased and he began smoothing up and down the back of her legs, her hips, her waist. He kissed the scented valley between her breasts, moving his face slowly from side to side, caressing her with his hair, his cheeks, his lips. The lazy, sensual savoringmade her tremble.

Luke turned his face once more and Carla felt the unexpected, velvet rasp of his mouth across the tip of her breast. Her breath fragmented into a moan of surprise and pleasure.

"I wanted to do this last night," Luke said, punctuating each word with teasing licks and tiny bites, "but I was too hungry for you."

Slowly he nuzzled the resilient, scented flesh, tasting Carla, tracing the line where smooth skin became textured velvet nipple. Sensations splintered through her as his tongue teased and tempted and shaped her. She sank her fingers into his hair and held him close, wanting to give herself to him, afraid that he would stop caressing her and turn away.

Luke's big hands smoothed down Carla's legs, then back up again. His long fingers flexed into her thighs, her hips, the graceful length of her back, kneading her with a slow, consuming sensuality that matched the rhythm of his mouth transforming her breasts into burning centers of sensation. After a long, long time he lifted his head and admired the flushed, glistening peaks.

"So beautiful," Luke murmured.

"Don't stop," Carla pleaded.

"Not a chance," he said, smiling with bittersweet acceptance. "I've hardly even begun."

He let the warmth of his breath rush over one sensitized breast. The tip of his tongue touched the hard nipple and then circled her in a tender caress that made her tremble. His tongue tasted her again, delicately, before his teeth closed on her with exquisite care. The whimper that came from her lips owed nothing to pain, everything to the pleasure that was licking over her in shimmering cascades of fire.

"I've wanted to do this since I saw you run in from a rain shower with your shirt sticking to you and your nipples standing up so proud and hard," Luke said huskily, turning to Carla's other breast, taking its peak into his warm mouth.

"Why didn't you?" She shivered with pleasure. "I wouldn't have minded."

"You were barely sixteen."

Carla's body stiffened in shock. "You wanted me that long ago?"

"Yes," he whispered, burying his face in her breasts, turning his head caressingly from side to side. "I wanted you until I could have screamed with it. But I shoved it down, buried it, ignored it, because I wanted something else even more."

"My brother's friendship?" Carla guessed.

"And yours." Luke kissed the swollen pink tip of first one breast, then the other. "When you and Cash were on the Rocking M, it was as close to a real family as I ever came. I needed that more than I needed sex.''

''You can have both now.''

''It doesn't work that way, sunshine,'' Luke whispered, his eyes narrowed against memories. ''Not on the Rocking M.''

Before Carla could ask Luke what he meant, one lean hand slid between her legs, seeking the softness that was concealed by dark curls. Her thoughts scattered as she felt again the gentle, probing caress of his fingertips. When he tested her silken depths, his name rushed between her parted lips in a startled cry as her knees gave way.

A few instants later Carla found herself back on the sleeping bag with Luke smiling down at her.

''You look surprised,'' he murmured. ''Didn't anyone ever warn you that your knees can give way?''

''I didn't believe them,'' she admitted huskily. ''I do now. You turn my bones to honey.''

Luke's eyes closed and his breath came in with a swift, husky sound as he bent over Carla and whispered, ''Turn to honey for me. Let me taste your sweetness.''

He kissed the sensitive curves of her ears, of her lips, of her breasts. Her navel fascinated him. He returned to the shadowed dimple again and again, probing with the sleek tip of his tongue, biting gently, making her moan with the unexpected sensations radiating out from her core. His caresses were like raindrops, a brushing of his mouth over her skin and then another brush and another until sensations overlapped and ran together, no beginning and no end, just heat gathering and rippling over her body, making her twist in slow motion as pleasure gathered, filling her until she moaned.

The touch of his tongue and the edge of his teeth on her legs came as a surprise and a very sharp pleasure. The warm pressure of his palms parting her thighs was another kind of caress, another kind of pleasure. When he pressed harder in silent request, asking that she open herself to him, she gave herself with a graceful abandon that nearly undid him. Slowly he bent down, tasting her with an intimate caress that made her cry out in surprise and passion.

"It's all right," Luke murmured, brushing the sensitive inner surface of Carla's thighs with his cheeks, gentling her even as his teeth took tiny, tiny bites of her softness. "You're all honey," he breathed against her. "So sweet. Don't fight me, sunshine. Let me have you this way. No risk, no pain, just...this."

The melting caress Luke gave Carla tore a wild, low cry from her throat. He traced her softness very lightly, silently coaxing and reassuring her. Then his caresses changed, urging her rather than seducing, demanding rather than gentling, consuming her in a shattering intimacy that brought her to ecstasy again and again, his dark words and her rippling cries blending with the falling rain, until finally she lay spent and trembling in the aftermath of wild ecstasy.

Only then did Luke lay beside Carla, hold her, gently kiss the tears from her eyelashes.

"Don't do this to me again, sunshine," Luke whispered, not knowing if Carla heard. *"Please. Don't."*

15

Even weeks later, the memory of that morning in September Canyon made Carla's breath catch. Luke had given her so much and had taken nothing for himself. Nor had he allowed her to give him anything in return. When she had calmed enough to draw a breath without having it break into fragments, he had stood up and walked out into the rain, leaving her alone with the echoes of his whispered plea.

Don't do this to me again, sunshine. Please. Don't.

Luke had done everything possible to make certain neither one of them was tempted into revisiting the passionate landscape of their dreams. He worked long days out on the range, getting up before dawn and rarely returning to the big house before ten o'clock. At meals he spoke to Carla when courtesy or necessity required it. Beyond that he said nothing to her.

And he walked across the room to avoid touching her.

At first Carla had thought that Luke's deliberate distancing of himself from her would pass, that he would allow himself to talk to her, to touch her, to be touched by her in more than physical ways. But hours had become days and days had become weeks. Luke hadn't relented. If anything, he had become more accomplished at evading even the remote chance of being alone with her. Day after day he eluded her until all her days on the Rocking M were gone.

Even today, the last one she was supposed to spend on the ranch. Tomorrow Carla was scheduled to leave the Rocking M. Tomorrow she was supposed to turn her back on a lifetime of dreams and the man she loved.

Why won't Luke even talk to me? Doesn't he know I love him? Doesn't he know I'm not like his mother or his aunts? Why won't he even give us a chance?

Tonight I've got to talk to him. Somehow I've got to make him understand. I can't leave tomorrow with this polite distance between us, as though September Canyon were only a dream and now I'm awake, aching...

The sound of something boiling over on the stove brought Carla out of her unhappy thoughts. She turned the gravy off and began mopping up. The burner hissed angrily at the touch of the cloth while she worked. Just as she finished, the back door slammed and the sound of booted feet rang in the silence.

Carla spun around with a hope she couldn't wholly conceal, any more than she could hide her disappointment that it was Ten rather than Luke. Even so, she smiled in greeting, putting aside her unhappiness as she always did when other people were around. But she was slower to conceal her feelings today, and her smile wasn't quite steady.

"Hi," Carla said. "There's nothing heavy to lift off the stove tonight."

"Then I'll just steal a cup of coffee," he said, watching her intently.

"Is something wrong?" she asked.

"I was just going to ask you the same question."

"Everything's fine. Dinner will be on time and big enough to feed an army."

"That isn't what I meant." Ten hesitated, swore under his breath and said bluntly, "You look unhappy."

"I'm always unhappy to be leaving the Rocking M," Carla said, her voice as matter-of-fact as she could make it. "Don't you remember? I used to pitch a regular fit when it was time to go back to Boulder."

"You were going back to school, then. What are you going back to now?"

"Actually, I'm going to help Cash wrestle with

his doctoral thesis. He's a whiz at cards and hard rock mining, but typewriters frustrate him.''

Ten started to say something, thought better of it and shrugged. "We're sure going to miss you.''

"Thanks." Unshed tears scorched Carla's eyelids. Impulsively she gave Ten a hug. "I'll miss you, too.''

Ten wrapped his arms around Carla, lifting her off the floor in a bear hug just as the back door slammed again.

"Put her down."

The tone of Luke's voice made Carla stiffen. Automatically she moved to end the hug. Ten's arms tightened, holding her captive. With a taunting lack of speed, Ten lowered Carla's feet to the floor, released her and turned to confront Luke.

"Something wrong, boss?"

Carla winced. She had learned that Ten only used the word "boss" when he thought Luke was out of line.

"Dinner is ready," she said quickly to Luke. "I'll set an extra plate. I wasn't expecting you.''

"I figured that out right away," Luke drawled coolly, "when I walked in and found you practicing your newfound techniques on my ramrod. Let me give you a bit of advice, schoolgirl. Ten doesn't like being tripped and beaten to the floor any more than I do.''

The sardonic words caught Carla completely unprepared. Luke had been so polite to her since September Canyon, so proper and distant. Not by so much as a word or a look had he alluded to what had passed between them; and now he was all but saying she had thrown herself at him and he had been unhappy at the result.

"Speak for yourself, boss man," Ten drawled, his voice every bit as cool as Luke's. "If Carla is in the mood to trip me, I'll fall to the floor any way she wants me."

"I didn't mean the hug that way," she said unhappily, watching both men, her face pale.

"Hell, I know that, honey," Ten said without looking away from Luke. "It's the boss who's a little thick between the ears where you're concerned."

"Don't kid yourself, ramrod. She may look as innocent as—"

"If you say any more," Ten interrupted curtly, "you'll regret it."

"Oh? And I suppose you're going to make me all regretful?" Luke asked.

"I won't have to. You'll look in the mirror and your stomach will turn over."

Ten's quiet certainty was more effective than a blow. Luke closed his eyes for a long count of three. When his eyes opened again they were no longer a savage, glittering gold. They were nearly opaque, full of shadows, as dull as gold could be. Ten muttered something sad and savage under his breath, but before either man could say anything more, the sound of the ranch hands gathering in the yard came through the open door.

"Find somebody else to give you the beating you think you deserve, Luke," Ten said softly. "I like you too well to enjoy hammering on you." He turned to Carla. "Go wash your face, honey, or you'll be answering a lot of questions about those tears."

Carla fled without a word.

When she came back, dinner was on the table and Luke was nowhere in sight. Ten looked up and smiled encouragingly at her.

"Told you she was just slicking up to impress us," he drawled to the table at large. "Nice job, honey. You look good enough to eat."

"Then it's a good thing for me you're already working on seconds, isn't it?" she said, smiling in return.

Only Ten noticed that Carla's smile hovered on the brink of turning upside down, and he wasn't going to point it out. He stood, pulled out her chair and seated her with easy grace.

"Thank you," Carla said, glancing up into his gray eyes as he bent over her. Quietly she added, "You're a good man, Ten. I don't know why some woman hasn't snaffled you off."

"One did," Ten murmured as he sat down again next to Carla. "It was a lesson to both of us."

"Hey, ramrod," Cosy said, jerking his thumb toward Luke's place. "The boss came in early today. Should I drag him out of the barn to eat?"

"Depends on how lucky you feel."

Cosy hesitated. "Uh-oh. You mean he's in the shop?"

"Yeah."

"Turning big hunks of wood into little bitty shavings?"

"Yeah."

"Is the door locked?"

"Yeah."

Cosy settled more deeply into his chair. "You gonna keep those potatoes for yourself or are you gonna share them with the hands what do the real work?"

Smiling thinly, Ten passed the potatoes.

"What are you two talking about?" Carla asked Ten.

The ramrod hesitated, then shrugged. "When things get to grinding too hard on Luke, he goes to his wood shop in the barn and locks the door behind him. You know that bed and dresser and table in your room?"

"I've been trying to figure a way to spirit the bedroom set out of the house when I leave," she admitted. "I've never seen any furniture one-tenth so beautiful."

"Luke made each piece three years ago. He worked all summer, way into the night, night after night, and then put in long days of ranch work every day, as well. After a few weeks of that he looked like hell, so I decided to talk some sense into him.'' Ten shook his head ruefully. ''That's a mistake I won't make twice. I'd as soon take on a cornered cougar with a licorice whip as tackle Luke when he's holed up in his workshop.''

Carla's uncertain appetite faded entirely as she digested Ten's words. Three years ago she had offered herself to Luke with unhappy results for both of them: *I've regretted that night like I've never regretted anything in my life.* So he had locked himself in his workshop and dealt with his emotions by creating an extraordinary bedroom set and putting it into a room no one used. Three weeks ago she had offered herself to Luke once more…and when it was over, he had whispered, *Please don't do this to me again.*

Now Luke had locked himself away once more, and he wasn't going to come out. Not while Carla was still on the Rocking M. She was sure of it. She was also certain she couldn't let that happen. She loved Luke too much to walk away and pretend that nothing had occurred between them except a one-night stand that never should have happened.

''Don't do it, honey,'' Ten said too softly for anyone but Carla to hear. ''Don't be the one to give Luke the fight he's looking for. You'll both regret it.''

Carla's head snapped up. She stared at Ten, startled by his accuracy in reading her thoughts.

"But I love him," she whispered.

"That just makes you more vulnerable."

"Luke came in early today. Maybe he wanted to talk to me. Maybe he..." Carla's voice frayed over the hope she couldn't put into words.

Maybe he wanted to ask me to stay.

The rest of the meal was a blur to Carla. She pretended to eat but only rearranged food on her plate. She looked attentive, but her thoughts went frantically around and around, trying to find a way past Luke's refusal to talk to her.

Afterward, when the table was clean and the kitchen was spotless and Luke still hadn't come back to the house, Carla went up to her room and began the unhappy task of packing. In the hope of luring him out of the barn, she carried out her luggage and boxes and loaded everything noisily into her little truck. It was a tight fit; because rain threatened, she was stuffing everything into the passenger side of the tiny cab.

No one came out of the barn while Carla arranged and rearranged boxes in the truck's small space. The men who poked their heads out of the bunkhouse and offered to help her were politely refused. She made many unnecessary trips, taking up as much time as possible, but finally she had no more excuses to linger around the yard and cast hopeful, sideways glances at the barn.

Carla went upstairs and washed her hair during a leisurely shower, hoping if she weren't downstairs,

Luke would feel free to come into the house. The instant she stepped out of the bathroom, she knew that Luke hadn't come in from the barn. There were no small sounds of someone stirring around the kitchen warming food or pouring coffee or washing up. There was simply silence and darkness and the distant flare of lightning dancing over MacKenzie Ridge.

Luke, don't send me away like this, not a word, nothing but silence. Talk to me. Give me a chance.

Nothing came in answer to Carla's plea but summer thunder, a reverberation more felt than heard.

Carla went to the dresser, opened the box Luke had carved for her and picked up the pottery fragment within. It was cool and hard and smooth, as though time itself had condensed in her palm. For long, long minutes she stood motionless, infusing ancient clay with the living warmth of her own body, holding the shard as though it were a talisman against her deepest fears. Finally, gently, she replaced the shard and packed the box into the overnight case that was her only remaining bit of luggage.

The sheets were as cool as the Anasazi fragment had been. Carla lay between them and waited to hear Luke's footsteps coming up the stairs.

The storm came first, a sudden, sweeping tumult riding on the back of a wild wind. Carla listened to all the voices of the storm, the high keening of the wind and the bass response of thunder, the sudden

crackle of lightning and the liquid drumroll of rain.
In between she heard the sound of Luke's footsteps
coming up the stairs. He passed her door without a
pause. The noise of the bathroom shower blended
seamlessly with the falling rain—long and hard and
relentless. Both shower and rain stopped with no
warning. In the silent spaces between peals of
retreating thunder, random creakings of the floor-
boards told Carla that Luke was prowling the con-
fines of bedroom and bath, bedroom and bath and
back again, ceaselessly.

Carla lay and listened, her hands clenched at her
sides, her whole mind caught up in a single, silent
plea: *Come to me, Luke. Once, just once, can't you
come to me?*

The footsteps came down the hall and passed her
bedroom door after a hesitation so small she
couldn't be sure she hadn't imagined it. The stairs
creaked, telling her that he was walking toward the
kitchen.

Walking away from her.

Carla waited and waited, but the footsteps didn't
return. Anger came to her as suddenly as the rain-
storm had come to the land. With a sweeping motion
of her arm, she threw the bed covers aside and stood
trembling, flooded with adrenaline and determination.

I'll make him listen to me.

Wearing only the black shirt Luke had left with
Cash and she had never returned, Carla went down

the hall on soundless bare feet. The only light on in the house came from the kitchen, but it was enough to illuminate the stairs. She took them in a rush.

Luke wasn't in the kitchen as Carla had expected. He was in the dining room, his chair turned away from the table, his elbows on his knees, a cup of forgotten coffee cooling on the table beside him. He was barefoot, wearing half-fastened jeans with nothing beneath but the desire that had made sleep impossible.

When Luke's eyes met hers, Carla felt as though she had touched bare electrical wire. His eyes had the feral blaze of a cornered cougar.

"Go back to bed, schoolgirl. Go now."

"We have to talk."

"Why? Are you pregnant?" he demanded, giving voice to the thought that had haunted him, his baby growing inside Carla's body, the sad history of the Rocking M repeating itself all over again after he had vowed that it would end with him.

Yet he wanted that baby with a yearning that was as deep as his need for Carla. Being torn between what he wanted and what he knew he must not have was making him wild. He could take no more—especially when she stood in front of him, wearing his shirt, her eyes luminous and her body etched in fire on his senses.

"It's not that," Carla said impatiently, determined not to be distracted from the main issue, which was Luke's determination not to face what was between them. "It's your refusal to—"

Luke's temper flashed at Carla's casual dismissal of the very pregnancy that had haunted him. He cut off her words with the same kind of attack that had once driven her away from the Rocking M and him. But not far enough. Not long enough.

This time he had to make it stick.

"Then why are you here?" he asked coldly. "You want more sex? Forget it. I was damn lucky not to get you pregnant in September Canyon. I'm not a fool to fall into the same trap twice. Sex isn't worth it."

But Carla was no longer a girl to flee from a man's anger. She held her ground despite the pain of his words twisting through her.

"That wasn't sex," she said. "It was love."

"It was sex," Luke countered savagely. "That's all men and women feel for each other. Plain old lust, schoolgirl."

"Some men. Some women," Carla agreed. She walked slowly toward him, fingers shaking slightly as she undid the top button of the black shirt, then a second, then a third. Her whole body was trembling with an urgency that was the other face of desire. She had to make him understand. She simply had to. "But not everyone is like that. I love you, Luke."

"Do you? Then button up and leave me in peace."

"But you won't be in peace. You'll be aching. You want me. You can't deny it, Luke. The evidence is right in front of you for both of us to see."

He said a single, harsh word.

She smiled sadly. "That's the general idea, but in our case it's called making love."

"I don't love you."

Carla's step faltered but didn't stop. She gathered her courage and continued to stalk her cornered cougar.

"I don't believe you," she said.

When her fingers undid the final button, the shirt parted to reveal the very feminine curves beneath. Luke's breath came in swiftly as her body was revealed and then concealed with each motion of the long, open shirt. He tried to look away, but couldn't. She was his own dream walking toward him, calling to him, her voice as much a part of him as his soul.

"Don't do this, baby."

"You're a big, strong man," Carla said, kneeling between Luke's long legs. "If you don't love me, prove it. *Stop me.*"

Her challenge was as unexpected to Luke as the feeling of his jeans coming suddenly undone, revealing the hard proof of his desire. He grabbed her wrists and dragged her hands upward, away from his hungry body.

It was a mistake. Even as her fingers tested the power of his clenched chest muscles, her hair fell across his hot, erect flesh in a silken caress. Before he had recovered from the shock, he felt the tip of her tongue in a soft, incendiarytouch.

If he hadn't already been sitting down, the savage torrent of his own response would have brought him to his knees. A harsh sound was ripped from his throat as every muscle in his big body clenched with the violence of his passion. He held her wrists with bruising force, but neither he nor she knew it. They knew only that the world was ablaze and they were the burning center of fire.

Between each sleek caress, each glide of velvet tongue against satin skin, Carla whispered her love to Luke; and somewhere between initial refusal and final acceptance, his hands released her wrists and his fingers threaded into her hair, caressing and holding and teaching her with the same aching motions. Every breath he took was her name, every heartbeat a hammering demand, his body hot, shimmering with leashed passion until he groaned harshly and could take no more. He lifted her, fitted her over himself and gave her what she had demanded, burying his hungry flesh in her, filling her with the sultry pulse of his ecstasy until the wild, shuddering release was finally spent and he could breathe once more.

"Think about this when I'm gone," Carla said, kissing Luke's eyelids, his cheeks, tasting the salt of passion glistening on his skin. "Think about this and remember what it was like to be loved by me. Then come to me, Luke. I'll be waiting for you, loving you."

16

"When are you going to stop this foolishness and call him?" Cash demanded from the hallway of Carla's apartment. His tone was divided between exasperation and concern, as was the look he gave her.

Carla glanced from the enigmatic shard of pottery lying in her palm to the dresser where the telephone sat in a silence that hadn't been broken for ten weeks. Slowly she looked at the twilight-blue color of Cash's eyes as he walked into her bedroom. His usual easy smile was absent and his jawline looked frankly belligerent. His sun-streaked, chestnut hair was awry, making its indomitable natural wave all the more pronounced.

"Call who?" she asked.

"Santa Claus," Cash retorted.

"It's a bit early for Christmas lists."

"It's nearly Thanksgiving and you've been home since the end of August."

Carla's slender fingers curled protectively around

the pot shard. She said nothing. She could count as well as her brother could. Better. She knew to the day when she had become pregnant: the last day on the Rocking M, when she had risked everything on one last throw of the dice.

And lost.

"Well?" demanded Cash.

"Well what?"

"When are you going to call Luke?"

Very gently Carla replaced the shard in its hand-carved nest, closed the lid and put the box on the dresser.

"I'm not."

"What?" Cash said.

"I'm not going to call Luke. I've chased the poor man for seven years. Don't you think it's time I left him in peace?"

Uneasily Cash assessed his sister's expression. Carla had grown up since the beginning of summer. Though she had said nothing specific, the sadness underlying her smiles told Cash that the summer hadn't worked out the way he had expected. What he didn't know was why.

"Luke has been fascinated by you for years, but you were too young," Cash said with his customary bluntness. "By the time you were old enough, he had made a habit of pushing you away. To make it worse, he has this fool idea that the Rocking M destroys women, and he loves that ranch the way most men love a woman. So I threw in a set of winning hands and sent you off for a summer of cooking on the Rocking M, where Luke could see for himself that you weren't going to fold up and cry just because you couldn't get your nails done every two weeks.''

Surprise replaced sadness in Carla's face. ''You set me up with that card game?''

''You bet I did. I thought the summer would give you two a chance to get acquainted with each other as adults, without me around to remind either of you about the years when you were a young girl in braids with a massive crush on a man who was old enough and decent enough to keep his hands in his pockets!''

''It worked,'' Carla said neutrally. ''You weren't around to remind us.''

''Like hell it worked. We're back to where we were three years ago, with Luke meeting me in West Fork for cards and beer and asking sideways questions about how you are and if you're dating and do I like any of the men you bring home.''

Carla closed her eyes so that Cash wouldn't see the wild flare of hope his words had given to her. The hope was as unreasonable as her seven years of longing for a man who didn't love her had been.

''Luke is just making polite conversation,'' Carla said, her voice soft in an effort to hide her pain. ''If he really wanted to know about me, he would pick up a phone and ask me himself.''

''That's what I told him the last time he asked.''

She smiled sadly. "And the phone hasn't rung, has it?"

"So make it ring. Call him."

"No."

The word was soft, final.

"Then I will."

"Please, Cash. Don't."

"Give me one good reason why I shouldn't."

"I don't want you to."

"That's emotion, not reason. Give me a reason, Carla. I'm fed up with watching the two people I love walking around half-alive. I was looking forward to a wedding at the end of summer, not a damned funeral!"

A single look at Cash's face told Carla that she wasn't going to win this argument. Her brother's easy smile and warm laughter concealed a steel core that was as deep and as hard as Luke MacKenzie's.

"Would you settle for being an uncle?" she asked softly.

"What?"

"I'm pregnant."

A shuttered look settled over Cash's face as he absorbed Carla's words. "Are you sure?"

"Yes."

"Does Luke know?"

"No."

Cash grunted. "I didn't think so. If he knew, I'd have a brother-in-law damned quick, wouldn't I?"

"No."

There was a long silence while Cash waited for Carla to explain. She said nothing.

"Talk to me," Cash said curtly. "I trusted Luke. Tell me why I shouldn't go out to the Rocking M and beat that son of a bitch within an inch of his life."

"It wasn't Luke's fault."

"That's bull, Carla! He's old enough to keep his hands in his pockets, and he damn well knows how babies are made or not made! Any man who seduces a virgin should have the decency—"

"He didn't seduce me," Carla said, cutting across her brother's angry words. "I seduced him."

"What?"

"I seduced Luke MacKenzie!" Carla yelled, letting go of her pride and her temper in the same instant. "I came up on his blind side, took off my clothes and made him an offer he couldn't refuse!" She took a deep, sawing breath and said more calmly, "So if you feel you have to beat somebody for a breach of trust, beat me."

Cash opened his mouth. No words came out. He cleared his throat and asked carefully, "And afterward?"

"Luke felt obliged to get married. I refused."

"Why?"

It was Carla's turn to be shocked into silence. It passed quickly, driven out by the same unflinching determination that had kept her from picking up the phone and calling Luke.

"I'll tell you why, brother dear. I'll go trout fishing in hell before I marry a man who doesn't love me."

"Don't be ridiculous. Luke loves you. Hell, he's loved you for years."

Tears came suddenly to Carla's eyes. She tried to speak but was able only to shake her head slowly while she fought for self-control.

"Lust," she said finally, her throat so tight she could barely squeeze the word out. "Not the same, Cash. Not the same at all."

"I don't believe you," Cash said flatly.

He reached past her for the telephone. Both of her hands clutched his wrist in a contest of strength that she couldn't possibly win.

"Then believe this," she said, her voice shaking. "If you tell Luke I'm pregnant I'll get in my truck and drive and keep on driving until I'm sure neither one of you will ever find me!"

"But, honey, you're pregnant. Be reasonable."

"I am. I'm not a charity case. I don't need a mercy marriage."

Cash flinched.

Too late, Carla remembered her brother's brief, unhappy marriage to a girl pregnant with another man's child.

"I'm sorry. I didn't mean that as a slap at Linda. She did what she believed she had to do." Carla put her arms around Cash and hugged him. "And your taking me in after Mom and Dad died ruined any chance you and Linda had. It also taught me that a man's sense of honor and decency is no substitute for love in a marriage. If Luke loved me, he would have called by now. He hasn't. Now it's up to me to pick up the pieces of my life. It's not Luke's problem, Cash. It's mine."

Cash kissed Carla's forehead, hugged her in return and said softly, "Honey, I'm as sure that Luke loves you as I am that I love you."

"Don't," she whispered, her voice aching with suppressed emotion. "You'll just make me cry. I miss him so much. It's like dying to know that he—he doesn't—doesn't—"

The shudder that racked Carla's body was transmitted instantly to her brother. His arms tightened around her.

"Go ahead and cry, honey," Cash whispered, closing his eyes, putting his cheek against Carla's hair, holding her. "Cry for both of us. And for Luke. Cry for him most of all, because he lost the most."

For a long time Cash held his sister, stroking her hair slowly, letting her cry out all the years of dreams that hadn't come true. When she had finally calmed, he kissed her cheek and released her.

"I'm not sure what I'm going to do about this," Cash said, pulling a handkerchief from his pocket and wiping away Carla's tears. "But I know what I'm *not* going to do. I'm not going to pick up the phone today and tell Luke you're pregnant. I interfered once with the two of you, and it blew up in everyone's face.''

Cash put the handkerchief in Carla's hand and wrapped her fingers around it.

"But, honey, once you start showing, someone's sure to mention it to Luke. Then there will be blazing red hell to pay." Cash hesitated, then added softly, "If you don't tell him by Christmas, I'll have to do it for you."

What Cash didn't put into words was his belief and fervent prayer that Luke surely would have called Carla by then.

17

A cold wind howled down from MacKenzie Peak, a wind tipped with the promise of sleet or snow. A gust caught Ten halfway between the bunkhouse and the barn. He ducked his head, pulled up the collar of his shearling jacket and went in the side entrance to the barn. The room he headed for had once held harness for the Rocking M's wagon horses. Now the room held woodworking tools—and a man who wielded them the way a wizard wields incantations against vicious demons.

The door had been locked since the evening Carla McQueen had driven off the Rocking M. After Luke had spent a long day working on the ranch, he would spend the evening and too much of the night locked inside the room, where the scream of a power saw biting into wood filled the spaces between the cries of the winter wind.

Ten was the only man who dared to disturb Luke in his lair. Lately, even Ten was thinking the matter over three or four times before he raised his fist and rattled the door on its hinges, praying that a small bit of Christmas spirit had sunk into Luke's hard head.

"Telephone, Luke!"

"Take a message."

"I did."

"Well?"

"Cash wants to know if you've seen Carla."

The scream of the power saw ended abruptly.

"What?"

"You heard me."

"What makes him th—"

"How the hell should I know?" interrupted Ten. "You have questions, go ask Cash yourself. I'm damn tired of standing around in a cold barn yelling at a man who's too blind to find his butt with both hands and a mirror the size of a full moon!"

Luke yanked opened the door and gave Ten a hard look. Ten returned it with interest.

"Give it to me again, slowly," Luke said.

"Lord, how you tempt a man," Ten muttered. "Listen up, boss. Cash McQueen is on the phone. Carla is missing. He seems to think she came here."

"On the day before Christmas?"

"Maybe she has some Christmas cookies for the hands."

Luke gave Ten a disbelieving look.

"Well, she brought us cookies a few years ago," Ten said blandly. "Maybe she decided to do it

again. What other reason could she have for coming
all the way out here?''

Luke stepped out of the room, slammed the door
behind him, locked it, pocketed the key and stalked
into the house. The kitchen phone was off the hook,
waiting for him.

"Cash, what the hell is going on?''

"I hoped you could tell me. I had to overnight in
New Mexico. When I got back, I found a note from
Carla saying she had something to do at the Rocking
M. So I called, but Ten says she isn't around.''

"When did she leave?''

"She should have been at the ranch house hours
ago,'' Cash said bluntly.

"Maybe she decided to go somewhere else.''

"She would have called and left a message on
my answering machine.''

Luke sensed the presence of Ten behind him. He
turned and shoved the phone into his ramrod's hand.

"Talk to Cash,'' Luke said curtly.

"Where are you going?''

"To check the south road for tread marks left by
a baby pickup truck. If I'm not back in ten minutes,
you'll know I found tracks and kept going.''

"To where?''

"September Canyon.''

Muddy water shot up and out from the big
pickup's tires as Luke forded Picture Wash with un-

usual velocity. He told himself he was pushing so hard because he was worried about Carla being alone in the desolate canyon with a storm coming on. But he didn't believe the rational lie. He drove like hell on fire because he was afraid she would have come and gone before he got there.

What's the hurry, cowboy? he asked himself sardonically. *Nothing has changed. Nothing can change. You can't have both Carla and the Rocking M. Beginning and end of story.*

There was no answer but the power of Luke's hands holding the big truck to the rutted road at a speed that was just short of reckless. The turnoff into September Canyon was taken in a controlled skid that made the truck shudder.

Relief coursed through Luke when he saw Carla's tiny pickup parked near a clump of piñon. He stopped nearby, pulled on his jacket and began walking quickly toward the overhang. The rich golden light of late afternoon slanted deeply across the canyon, heightening every small crevice in the cliffs and every tiny disturbance of the soil, making the land look as though it had been freshly created.

There was no sign that Carla had been beneath the overhang since August. There were no fresh ashes in the fire ring, no new tracks near the seep's clean water, no sleeping bag stretched out and waiting for the night that would soon descend.

I was right. She isn't planning to stick around.

The realization sent a cold razor of fear slicing

through Luke. The feeling was irrational, yet it couldn't be denied.

I could so easily have missed her. Why didn't she tell me she was coming? Why did she drive all the way out to the Rocking M and not even say hello?

No sooner had the questions formed than their answers came, echoes of a summer and a passion that never should have been, Carla's voice calling endlessly to him, haunting even his dreams: *Remember what it was like to be loved by me. Then come to me, Luke. I'll be waiting for you, loving you.*

But he hadn't gone to her. He had gone instead to the old harness room. There he had transformed his yearning, his pain and his futile dreams into gleaming curves of wood, pieces of furniture to grace the family life he would never have.

Wind curled down through the canyon, wind cold with distance and winter, wind wailing with its passage over the empty land. The overhang took the wind, muffled it, smoothed it, transformed it into voices speaking at the edge of hearing and dreams, a man and a woman intertwined, suspended between fire and rain, their cries of fulfillment glittering in the darkness.

Abruptly Luke knew why Carla hadn't set up camp beneath the overhang. She could no more bear its seething not-quite-silence than he could.

It took only a few moments for Luke to find the tracks Carla had left when she headed up the canyon. Her footprints followed the trail markers she

had left in August. All other signs of her previous
visit had been washed away by rain. Luke walked
quickly, fighting the impulse to run, to overtake the
girl who had left nothing more of herself in September Canyon than a fragile line of tracks that
wouldn't outlive the next winter storm.

Filled with an anxiety that he neither understood
nor could control, Luke scrambled up the narrow
tongue of rock and debris that looked out over the
canyon. There was no one waiting at the top, no girl
with blue-green eyes and a smile that set a man to
dreaming of marrying one special woman, having a
family with her, watching their children grow to
meet the challenges of the beautiful, unflinching
land.

"Carla?"

No answer came back but the haunted wind.

Luke looked around quickly for Carla's tracks but
found none. Where the surface wasn't gravel it was
solid rock. He glanced up the canyon, then down,
then up again. No one was in sight. He scrambled
down the far side of the promontory. There were no
rocks piled to mark the way, nothing to indicate
which direction Carla had taken. If she had left
tracks, the rich sidelight of the descending sun
would have made them stand out like flags.

"Damn it, Carla," he muttered, scanning the view
impatiently, "you know better than to take off without leaving any markers to—"

The angry words stopped when Luke's breath

came in fast and hard and stayed there. His head snapped around and he looked up canyon again. This time he saw nothing but rock, piñon, sunlight and shadow. Yet there had been something there before, a glimpse of right angles and rectangular shadows that were at odds with his expectations. Nature's geometry was circular, curve after curve flowing through unimaginable time. Man's geometry was angular, line after line marching through carefully divided time. He had seen a hint of man, not canyon.

Carefully he turned his head again. There, just at the corner of his vision, Luke glimpsed right angles and rectangular shadows tucked away amid September Canyon's graceful curves. Only the unusual angle of the sunlight allowed him to see the cliff house, for it was screened by trees and nestled in one of September Canyon's many side canyons. A chill moved over Luke as he realized that he was looking at the ruins of a cliff house that had been old when Columbus set sail for India and found the New World instead.

And within those stone ruins a hidden fire burned, sending a thin veil of smoke toward the cloud-swept sky.

As Carla had before him, Luke walked toward the ruins. Even knowing they were there, and having the richly slanting light as an aid, he found it difficult to locate the ruins once he looked away. He stopped, took his bearings from the canyon itself and walked toward the ruins with the confidence of a man accustomed to finding his own way over a wild land. He didn't call out to Carla; wind and silence were the only voices suited to hidden canyon.

Luke found Carla at the very edge of the ruins, sitting in an ancient room that had no ceiling. Enough of the walls remained to give shelter from the keening wind. The small fire she had built burned like a tiny piece of the sun caught amid the twilight of the ruins. She was staring into the heart of fire, her right hand curled into a fist. Tears shone like silver rain on her cheeks, a slow welling of sadness that made Luke's own throat ache.

"There's a storm coming on," he said, his voice husky with emotions he couldn't name. "You shouldn't camp here. There's not enough shelter. Why don't you come back with me?"

Carla turned and looked at the man whose child was growing within her body, the man she loved.

The man who didn't want her love.

"No, thank you," she said politely. "I don't want to impose on you."

A coolness moved over Luke's skin that had nothing to do with the swirling wind.

"That's ridiculous," he said. "You know you're always welcome on the Rocking M."

"Don't."

"Don't what?"

"Lie. I'm not welcome on the Rocking M and we both know it. You were relieved to wake up and find me gone."

"Carla—"

Luke's throat closed and the silence stretched while Carla watched him with blue-green eyes that were darker than he remembered. Then her lips curved in a small smile that was sadder than any tears he had ever seen.

"Don't worry, Luke. I'm not going to throw myself at you again. I've finally grown up. I'm as tired of being pushed away by you as you are of having to push me."

She laughed suddenly. The soft, broken sound made Luke flinch, but she didn't see it. She had opened her right hand and was staring at the fragment of ancient pottery that rested on her palm. Luke endured the silence as long as he could, then asked the only question he would allow himself.

"Did you find that here?"

A brief shudder went over Carla, but that was her only acknowledgment that she was no longer alone. Just when Luke began to wonder if she would answer, she spoke in a flat, colorless voice.

"You gave this to me seven years ago. I brought it back to the place where it belongs. Full circle."

Luke felt as though the world had dropped away from beneath his feet. Always in the past he had known with unspeakable, absolute certainty that Carla would come back to the Rocking M, to him, bringing sunshine and laughter and peace with her. He had come to count on that, hoarding memories of her like a miser counting jewels, knowing that one day he would look up and she would be there again, watching him with a love she had never been able to hide.

The realization of what had happened sank into Luke like a blade of ice, slicing through him even as it froze him, teaching him that he had never known pain until that moment. Carla had come back, but not to him. She would leave again.

And she would never come back.

"I'm selling the ranch."

Shocked by Luke's words, Carla looked up, facing him again. The pain she saw in his golden eyes made her feel as though she were being torn apart.

"But—why?"

"You know why."

With a small, anguished sound, Carla turned back to the fire, knowing that there was no more hope. All her dreams, all her love, everything was destroyed.

"Cash shouldn't have called you," she said hoarsely. "He promised me until Christmas."

Carla's fingers clenched around the pottery shard. The pain of it reminded her of why she had come to September Canyon. She drew back her arm to hurl the ancient shard back into the fire.

"No!" Luke said.

He moved with shocking speed, closing his much bigger hand around her fist, forcing her to hold on to his gift. Slowly he knelt in front of her, bringing her right hand to his lips despite her struggles.

"Don't leave me, sunshine," Luke said, kissing Carla's slender fingers. "Stay with me. Love me."

The words pierced Carla's last defenses, teaching her how little she had understood of pain until that moment. She couldn't breathe, couldn't speak; she could only be torn apart by the knowledge that it had all been for nothing, all the pain, all the loneliness, all the years of yearning.

And now he was pressing his lips against her fingers, pleading with her to stay, to give him the love he had always pushed away in the past. Now, when Cash had told Luke she was pregnant.

Now, when love was impossible.

Duty. Decency. Honor. Obligation. The words were colder than the wind, more massive than September Canyon's stone ramparts. The words were crushing her. She couldn't live a lifetime with Luke, knowing every time that she wasn't loved. She couldn't even live another instant that way.

"Let me go, Luke," Carla said, her voice breaking. "I can't bear being your obligation. I can't bear knowing the only reason you came to me at all is that Cash told you I'm pregnant."

"Pregnant!"

The dark center of Luke's golden eyes dilated with a shock that was unmistakable. With quick motions he unbuttoned her jacket.

"Didn't he—" Carla's voice broke as Luke's big hands went from her throat to her hips, discovering every change four months of pregnancy had made in her body.

"My God," Luke said again and then again, his voice ragged.

Slowly his hands moved over her, touching her in wondering silence because he could not speak.

"Cash didn't tell you?" Carla whispered, sensing the answer yet unable to help the words. She had to know. She had to be certain.

Luke shook his head.

"Then why—why did you come here?" she asked.

He took a deep, shuddering breath and said simply, "I had to."

Carla watched Luke with uncertain eyes, afraid to think, to hope. "I don't understand."

With a gentleness that made Carla tremble, Luke brushed his lips over the shining trails her tears had made on her cheeks. It was the first time he had ever kissed her without being asked; the realization was as devastating to Carla as the tenderness of his caresses. Without thinking, she raised her hand to push him away, unable to bear being hurt again.

"Don't," Luke said hoarsely. "Please don't push me away, sunshine. I know I deserve it, but I can't— oh, God, I can't bear losing you. When Cash told me you had come to the Rocking M, I went crazy. I knew you had come to September Canyon but I didn't know why. I hoped—I hoped so much you were coming back to me.

"And then you told me you were going to leave my gift here and never come back. *Full circle*. That's what you mean, isn't it? Leaving and never coming back to me again?"

Slowly Carla nodded.

Luke closed his eyes and fought to control the emotions clawing at him. "Until a few seconds ago," he said finally, "I thought I'd accepted the fact that I could have a family or I could have the Rocking M. I've realized it for years, since before I even knew you and Cash. I tried not to care, because I love this ranch more than I ever wanted any woman." Luke bent his head a bit more, tasted the tears shining on Carla's lips and felt his own eyes burn. "Then one day I looked at you and saw a woman I wanted to have children with..."

His voice went from husky to hoarse as emotion closed his throat. For long, sweet seconds he moved his hands gently over Carla's womb as though to caress the life within.

"I'd sworn never to sacrifice my woman and children to the Rocking M," he said. "I knew what this land did to women. I had heard about it, seen it, almost been destroyed by it when I was young."

Luke drew a quick, broken breath and fought for control. "Every time I looked at you, I was reminded of the truth," he whispered. "I could have the ranch or I could sell it and have you. So I pushed you away and hungered for you to come back, because as long as you came back I could have both you and the Rocking M. Do you understand?''

Carla tried to speak but all that came out was Luke's name, a ragged sound as painful as his voice.

"Don't cry," he whispered, kissing her gently, repeatedly, as though he could drink all the sadness from her with his lips, leaving her free of pain. "It's all right. When I realized you would never come to me again, the choice was easy. I can live without the Rocking M but I can't live with knowing I hurt you."

Luke tilted Carla's chin up until he could see her eyes. "Where do you want to live after we're married?"

"On the Rocking M."

Pain and a wild, flaring hope tightened Luke's features in the instant before he shook his head. "I'll never ask that of you."

"Do you believe I love you?"

"There could be no other reason for what you've done, giving me so much, asking for so little and getting even less. I'm sorry for that, baby. I'm so damned sorry. You deserved so much more from me."

Carla pulled Luke's head closer, returning the gentle kisses he had given her, loving him so much it was a sweet kind of pain.

"The Rocking M is part of you," she whispered between kisses. "If I hadn't loved the ranch, I couldn't have loved you. Not really. I could have had a schoolgirl crush on you. I could have been infatuated with you. I could have been fascinated by you. I could have been everything except in love with you. But I love the ranch, and I love you." Carla smiled suddenly, making the tears in her eyes sparkle like crystal in sunlight. "In fact, you should be worried that I'm marrying you *for* the Rocking M, not in spite of it."

"Sunshine," Luke said, his voice catching, "I want you to be happy. Are you sure?"

"As sure as I am pregnant."

He closed his eyes. "Are you happy about that?"

"Being pregnant?"

Luke's eyes opened. "Yes."

"Oh, yes," Carla murmured, covering his hands with her own, cradling him against the new life growing within her body. "Are you?"

"I can't—I don't—have words." Luke bent down and kissed her hands, then sought the warmer flesh beneath that sheltered his baby. "When you left, I shut myself in the barn and made a cradle and a crib and a rocking horse for the child I would never have. And then I made a—rocking chair so that you— could—" His voice broke. He tried to speak, but all that came out was a raw whisper. "I looked at the chair—and dreamed of you nursing our child—and knew it would never—never—"

Carla felt the shudders that ripped through Luke's control, felt the scalding heat of his tears against her skin and held him until she ached. For long minutes there was only the sound of his broken breathing and her own whispered words of love. Finally he stood up, carrying her with him, holding her as close as the beating of his own heart.

Then Luke looked down in Carla's clear eyes. He felt something shimmer through him like sunrise, transforming him, freeing him from the darkness of the past, giving him a vision of a future more beautiful than his hungry dream. He wanted to tell Carla all that he saw—a girl with dark hair and golden eyes and her mother's flashing smile, a boy with gentle hands and blue-green eyes and his father's easy strength, a man and a woman sharing and building and creating together, giving back to life the gift it had given them.

The vision was so clear to Luke, so real, beyond question or doubt. He wanted to share it with Carla, to tell her that neither one of them would ever be lonely again. Yet of all the gifts that had come to him, of all the truths yet to be given and received, only one came to his lips when he bent down to her, for it was the only truth that mattered.

"I love you, sunshine."

MONTANA MAVERICKS
Big Sky Brides

Legendary love comes to Whitehorn, Montana,
once more as beloved authors

Christine Rimmer, Jennifer Greene and Cheryl St.John

present three brand-new stories in this exciting anthology!

Meet the Brennan women:
SUZANNA, DIANA and ISABELLE

Strong-willed beauties who find unexpected
love in these irresistible marriage of
covnenience stories.

Don't miss
MONTANA MAVERICKS: BIG SKY BRIDES
On sale in February 2000,
only from Silhouette Books!

Available at your favorite retail outlet.

The clock is ticking for three brides-to-be in these three brand-new stories!

3, 2, 1... *Married!*

In this exciting collection of romantic tales, three marriage-minded women set their sights on becoming brides in time for the New Year.

How to hook a husband when time is of the essence?

Bestselling author **SHARON SALA** takes her heroine way out west, where the men are plentiful...and more than willing to make some lucky lady a "Miracle Bride."

Award-winning author **MARIE FERRARELLA** tells the story of a single woman searching for any excuse to visit the playground and catch sight of a member of "The Single Daddy Club."

Beloved author **BEVERLY BARTON** creates a heroine who discovers that personal ads are a bit like opening Door Number 3—the prize for "Getting Personal" may just be more than worth the risk!

On sale December 1999, at your favorite retail outlet.

Only from Silhouette Books!

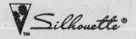

Celebrate Silhouette's 20ᵗʰ Anniversary

With beloved authors, exciting new miniseries and special keepsake collections, **plus** the chance to enter our 20ᵗʰ anniversary contest, in which one lucky reader wins the trip of a lifetime!

Take a look at who's celebrating with us:

DIANA PALMER
April 2000: SOLDIERS OF FORTUNE
May 2000 in Silhouette Romance: *Mercenary's Woman*

NORA ROBERTS
May 2000: IRISH HEARTS, the 2-in-1 keepsake collection
June 2000 in Special Edition: *Irish Rebel*

LINDA HOWARD
July 2000: MacKENZIE'S MISSION
August 2000 in Intimate Moments: *A Game of Chance*

ANNETTE BROADRICK
October 2000: a special keepsake collection, plus a brand-new title in
November 2000 in Desire

Available at your favorite retail outlet.

Where love comes alive™

(Answers: **Mostly A: Silhouette Romance;**
Mostly B: Silhouette Desire;
Mostly C: Silhouette Special Edition;
Mostly D: Silhouette Intimate Moments)

Series Descriptions:

SILHOUETTE ROMANCE:

Tender, heartwarming stories that will move you with the wonder of love. It's romance the way you always knew it could be.

SILHOUETTE DESIRE:

Passionate, powerful, provocative love stories featuring strong heroes and spirited heroines. Silhouette Desire captures the intensity of falling in love in sensuous romances that fulfill **your** every desire.

SILHOUETTE SPECIAL EDITION:

Complex and packed with emotion, these substantial novels are tales that you can identify with—romances with "something special" added in! Silhouette Special Edition is entertainment for the heart.

SILHOUETTE INTIMATE MOMENTS:

Enter a world where excitement is always high and passions run hot. Dramatic, larger than life and always compelling—Silhouette Intimate Moments provides an thrilling mix of passion, adventure and drama.

❦❦❦❦❦❦❦❦❦❦❦❦❦

What's Your Series? Free Book Offer!

The following series is the series that suits me the best
(Please check ONE).

Romance	Desire	Special Edition	Intimate Moments
CTR3 ❑	CTR4 ❑	CTR5 ❑	CTR6 ❑

PLEASE SEND MY FREE SAMPLE TO:

Name:

Address:

City: State/Province:

Zip/Postal Code:

The Right Romance!

Complete the quiz and send in for a FREE book!

With so many wonderful romance titles available, trying to figure out which ones will give you the most satisfaction can be downright daunting. But we've made it easy! Just take this quiz to find out which Silhouette line is the perfect one for you!

1. You're going to curl up on the couch with a blanket, a snack and your favorite movie on the VCR. It is:
    - (a) *While You Were Sleeping*
    - (b) *An Officer and a Gentleman*
    - (c) *Parenthood*
    - (d) *The Big Easy*

2. The song that best describes your life is:
    - (a) "Endless Love"
    - (b) "Light My Fire"
    - (c) "Having My Baby"
    - (d) "Secret Agent Man"

3. Your ideal mode of transportation is:
    - (a) a Saturn
    - (b) a Mustang convertible
    - (c) a minivan
    - (d) the Concorde

4. Your celebrity dream date would be:
    - (a) Tom Hanks
    - (b) Brad Pitt
    - (c) George Clooney
    - (d) Harrison Ford

5. The greatest gift your special someone could give you is:
    - (a) a bouquet of roses
    - (b) a sexy negligee
    - (c) a "his & her" day at the spa
    - (d) two tickets to Tahiti

Calculate your results on the following page...